What Happened to Kristopher on the Rose

Thank you to Dave Potts who edited
the final draft of this book.
He has skilfully corrected all my typing,
punctuation,
short-comings and illiteracy.
If mistakes remain
I am to blame by my lack of
diligence in transcribing his
alterations to the master copy.

Thanks to Nicola Emma
for her help on the first draft

What Happen to Kristopher On The Rose Tree Estate?

Cher Bonfis: - Was discovered at the back of a Glasgow Omnibus when the driver checked after a long shift. The baby was in a Moses basket, and, tucked into a pocket in the side of that basket was a magazine, the cover of which was adorned by a world famous pop singing star… No, sorry, that was a lie. Let us begin again… Cher was born on the night of a blue moon in a wee hospital in Aberlour right near to a famous biscuit factory….Sorry that was another lie….Not about the biscuit factory….Michael Finnegan begin again? Probably not, for the words written here, or in some newspaper, would not really allow you into the mind of this author. If you want to know about this person it is best that you read the things this person writes. Trivia over details of this life are irrelevant. What you should know is that there is much gratitude for your interest and there is hope that you have found something rewarding. If you believe in love and kindness. If you believe everyone deserves a chance to live a happy life then you and Cher Bonfis have a lot in common. Word by word we will strive to make things better. So thank you for stopping by, and may all good things be yours.

What Happened To Kristopher On The Rose Tree Estate?

Cher Bonfis

Lulach Publishing

PB

First published by Lulach Publishing in 2022

Lulach Publishing
https://www.lulachpublishing.com

Cher Bonfis
What Happened to Kristopher on The Rose Tree Estate?

British Library cataloguing in Publication Data. A Catalogue record for this book is available from the British Library.

ISBN: 978-1-7396723-0-0

BIC categories:- FA,

Typeset in
Elatan

A man of sixty-three years, Kristopher, seeks the help of a psychiatrist to ascertain what he has been hiding from himself for the past sixty years, since he lived on the notorious

Rose Tree Estate.

Which, was a group of children's care homes overseen by Borough Councils in London.

Sadly, as demonstrated by child abuse enquiries, children in the care of the state have not all be treated well. Many suffered greatly at the hands of their carers. The stories that appear in the media often reflect that small section of the life within care homes. This book aims to broaden the narrative and show both the bad and the good within these structures. The book also attempts to add an historical perspective. The story runs between nineteen thirty-five to around two-thousand and sixteen. The awful stories are always bought well to the fore, some of these are included in the book. There are also stories about the good people who did care, and who did their best to provide a loving home for those who needed it. Further, there are stories of those who grew up and went on to live enjoyable lives.

Kristopher's story is truly shocking.

This is a work of fiction.
The names or characters,
businesses or places,
events or incidents, are fictitious.
Any resemblance to actual persons,
living or dead, is purely coincidental.

"Suffer little children, and forbid them not.
To come unto me: for such is the kingdom of heaven."

The King James VI/I Bible: Matthew 19:14

PERFACE

In various locations, during most of the twentieth century, society in the United Kingdom introduced a solution, to what had been perceived as a problem, children who had no fit parents to care for them. There were thousands of young people who, every year, found themselves orphaned, or abused, or lost. Some children could not stay with their natural parents for many different reasons. Some washed up on the shore from other lands. Some children came into conflict with the law and required close supervision. So in the early part of the twentieth century societies set up villages. Houses were built, and staff employed and those who had nowhere else to go would be accommodated. Examples of such places, in the south of England, in Surrey and Kent. As the years rolled on the London County Council took on the responsibility for these places and, when that Council was abolished, Wandsworth and Lambeth Borough Councils took them on.

Atrocities occurred not only in England but in many other places too. One Scottish solicitor was working with survivors of eight different institutions.

Over the many years these places were in existence they provided a refuge for many. However, they also became places that harmed many others because of the behaviour of some of the carers and people who took advantage of the situation the children were in. Many media organisations have highlighted the appalling behaviour of those, and the devastation that was caused to fragile young humans who required love, kindness, and compassion not to become objects of sexual gratification.

These villages were 'full-on' communities, ecosystems in their own right. I know because I grew up in such places. Living in one of these places was, undoubtedly, a supremely unpleasant experience for many. However, to limit the conversation to the harm does not provide a full picture.

Whilst I hesitate to claim that this work will provide an absolutely full picture, it is an attempt to make the picture broader and deeper. For among those who did so much harm, there were others who did so much good.

This is a work of fiction based upon my own experiences; in various institutions, in which I lived, and upon stories I have listened to and read.

The following story will be told by Kristopher and a Narrator

CHAPTER 1

Session Ten: Incy-wincy Spider

Kristopher

The first thing the doctor wanted to know, during our first session, was. "What was the first thing I could remember learning?" I thought this was a strange thing to ask but he was insistent. I paused for a moment and then said this.

"Well learning in the sense that I was at nursery school and the 'teacher' had a group of us sitting on those little chairs, and we had to repeat after her....

'Incy-Wincy Spider climbing up the spout,
down came the rain and washed the spider out,
out came the sun and dried up all the rain,
and Incy-Wincy Spider climbed up the spout again.'

It could have been that, or one of numerous other rhymes. This one had a lot of hand actions and it is very clear to me."

The psychiatrist was twenty years younger than I, and although I had studied many books on motivation, and understood much about human behaviour, I felt uneasy. I had become a good salesman, with the things I had learned, but I knew that this doctor had knowledge of much deeper 'magic' than I. I could feel him probing deeply into my most hidden thoughts. This was our tenth session, and I could hear his skeleton keys jangling. I knew he was about to unleash the truly feared wild animals I had mentally secured in cages six decades ago. I was still fighting to keep him away from those cages, although I could no longer recall what was in them. I knew I did not want to confront whatever they were, which is why I kept them in the very darkest corridor in my mind. They had been there for so long I had, all but, forgotten they were there. The doctor was now so close, I could hear sounds of the ferocious beasts, screeching and roaring. It was as if he had syringed wax from my ears so that, once muffled, distant noises were now sharp clear tones. I did not want to get closer. There were beads of sweat on my forehead. The psychiatrist's office was dark, but warm, and so very quiet. The smell of the leather seat, which snuggled about me, gave me comfort, I clung to the armrests, like a mountain climber, hoping they would save me from the fall; but this doctor had charms, and incantations, which beguiled, they smashed through the defences that had secured so many horrors for so long. Although, I had no wish to confront these monsters, I knew there was going to be no choice. I might hold it off for this session, I might tell myself I will not turn up next time, but I knew that I was bewitched, and I knew that I had no choice, I had come so far, and like Charles Lindbergh, I had passed the point of no return and the Atlantic Ocean was beneath me.

*

Kristopher

The myth was, that the moon is made of cheese! An easy myth, at one time, for no one had a chance to debunk it. Then rocket ships went to the moon, and then Buzz Aldrin, and Neil Armstrong also went to the moon; they returned with some fragments, which no one could eat. Now we truly know that the moon is not made of cheese. Yet, in some minds, it will never be made of rock!

In the minds of some people live gods. Those people are controlled by those gods. There are some gods, which inhabit the minds of many people at the same time. Those gods have great power. Such power that massed, raging, armies are willing to set to war for the same god that they both believe in. Two sides, in one conflict, can believe that their god will secure victory, and even if their army looses they may still sing the god's praises even though the god favoured their opponent's army! Gods come and go, they provide mortals with fear and power. They make it possible for millions of humans to organise their world.

It can be difficult to dislodge a myth, from a group, or an individual. Here you are, peering at these words, and I am wondering if I can dislodge any myths which you may hold.

My name is Kristopher. I am sixty-three years old. This story began in nineteen fifty-eight and I was then just two and a bit years old. Some parts of this story, you may find, are dark and uncomfortable, when you realise exactly what happened you might well feel distressed.

You may well have to wrestle with some myths that you hold, deep, and dear. You may have to come to terms with the notion that gods and other myths are man-made. Mankind makes many problems in the battle between culture and nature. Nothing in nature is forbidden nothing in nature is unnatural. You may conclude that, sometimes, the unnaturalness of some natural things is abhorrent. You might want to thank culture for trying to save us from those things, which in nature can often be seen as reckless.

I hope that no one who reads this would wish or do harm to any child, or indeed to any person. Sadly there are people who cause vicious harms to those who are truly vulnerable. Do not be fooled into thinking this is going to be a simple story. No, this story is complex and made like a mosaic from thousands of bits of many different lives. We have begun with my tenth session with Doctor Samuels, and me remembering my first session with him. We will return to Session Ten much later in the book but now I will tell you of my first session with the good Doctor.

Chapter 2
Session One: Let us begin at the beginning
Kristopher

"It is generally believed that, if a person is born into a happy and secure environment, they are able to retain more memories from their earliest months. People who suffer, to any degree, in their early days, tend to retain fewer memories from those parts of their lives." replied the psychiatrist to my question during the first session. These sessions had been scheduled every fortnight, until what had happened was understood.

"So, please, Kristopher, give me a little bit of your family background. In your own time, no need to rush, I find details fascinating, and the more I know the easier it will be for you to understand, and come to terms with your feelings." said the doctor, somewhat pompously I thought, but I did not say that, for I barely knew the man, and besides he was, I had been informed, the best person for the job. Heavens! His fees were eye-watering, I thought, so that recommendation had better be sound.

I began to relate the biography of my life. I knew that the sessions were being recorded. I had not thought that I would transcribe them so that you could read them, but that is exactly what you are about to do.

*

"God Mad is how my granny described my mum. My mum claimed that she was an evangelical preacher. She met my dad whilst they were members of the Army of the Church. An oxymoron if ever there was one. Then they often sang that hymn which was made popular after Arthur Sullivan gave it a decent tune. Onward Christian Soldiers. Somehow the idea of fighting, soldiers, armies and war anathema to this so-called Christian idea. So why Army of the Church? A former soldier started it by bringing together some soldiers, officers and some working men and women. He trained them to become evangelists for Henry VIII's, three hundred and fifty year old, Church of England. Henry had long since vacated the throne by 1882, when this group descended upon the slums of Westminster. The idea was to get out into places where there were people who would never dream of entering a church. He held open-air services, and these people did what they could to help people and to spread their message, their version of their religion.

"Whilst we are on the subject of church, one of the reasons I fell out with religion was this. They say love thy neighbour as thyself. Well from my experience in life, doctor, I can tell you there are many, many people who do not love themselves very much at all. I would say that looking around there are many people who do not even like themselves. I remember someone saying to me 'You cannot give what you do not have'. If you do not love yourself, doctor, is it really possible to love other people? If you do not care for yourself is it possible to care for other people? Or, indeed, anything? I have a feeling that, as I tell you my stories, we will meet many people who did not know how to love themselves, because sadly, no one had loved them. You cannot give what you do not have."

The doctor said. "Yes I can see what you are getting at. Please Kristopher continue, you were telling me of your parents' days in the Army of the Church."

I continued. "Relationships between men and women members of this Army of the Church organisation were strictly forbidden. It was nineteen fifty-two."

I paused a moment for my thoughts to catch up with my mouth.

"What I am going to say next has really nothing to do with all of this, but I remember when I travelled to Islamic countries, if ever I were to see a television programme, the most brutal of acts of violence were openly shown, yet if a man and a women were about to show love for one another by kissing, suddenly the film would cut to the next scene. Violence and killing were OK, loving and kissing were not. Church and Army! Army it is just the wrong word in my thoughts."

The doctor responded. "Yes in a way it is a contradiction, but we do speak of an army of ants, for example."

"At Christmas; my dad told me this story more than once. All Army of the Church members went off to their respective families and friends, ensuring that their contact details, for the duration of the holidays, were logged. My dad wrote in the logbook that he would be staying with his pal Simon, who later became my godfather, however, my dad boarded a train to the hometown of the girl he had fallen in love with, another Army of the Church member, the woman who would, in time, become my mother. He stayed at her house, with her family instead of staying with Simon. He had not thought that anyone would check up on him, but they did! The result was that my mum, to be, had to resign her position. Insubordination; maybe there is a gene, which was passed to me!"

Doctor Samuels made a note and then asked. "So you consider yourself to be insubordinate Kristopher? He did not let me answer; he just said, "I see. Please carry on."

I actually had never thought of it in that way. Doctor Samuels had interrupted what I had said, but my thoughts were on the move, and they could not go back and argue.

"My dad had grown up in Uganda, he was a Boy Scout his father drove the railway trains in East Africa. My dad spent the last part of the Second World War in the RAF. Later, during his National Service, he patrolled the streets of Palestine, with his rifle; and spent some time in Madagascar, which was the only mention, dad gave to the subject of military service.

Whilst in the air-force, during the time he spent Palestine, he said, he had encountered God in a vision of light. He took his ambition to become a minister to the Bishop who told him to go and live a little bit first.

"So at the end of his National Service, at his demob, he realised that he could get a free passage to England, if he demobbed in England rather than Africa. No one seemed to notice that his request was not strictly correct. He stood on the station at Nairobi, in Kenya, and heard his name called out over a loud speaker; he thought he had been rumbled. As it turned out there were two people, on the platform, with the same name, so he managed to journey all the way to England for free. He never returned to Africa, Uganda or Kenya."

"I take it that you admired your father, and that you had great affection for him?" Interrupted Doctor Samuels. He made another note on the paper which was affixed to an aluminium clipboard. The doctor used a gold fountain pen, which reflected any ray of light with splendour. "Please continue Kristopher."

At first these interruptions disturbed me, but actually, as they became familiar, they made me feel as if this man was really listening to me, I felt he was really interested, the interruptions made me think a bit more about what I had said, and what I was going to say. Sometimes they gave me a chance to remember details, which I may not have included. I think that Doctor Samuels used these interruptions to put me at my ease. They became the basis of the relationship we built. The interruptions turned my monologue into something of a conversation. At one point Doctor Samuels said he had noted that, despite my education, my affection for my father and mother, which would be the way people might have expected me to speak of them, if they only heard my accent, made me always call them 'dad' and 'mum'. Something I had never thought of. I continued with the history of my dad and mum.

"My folks were married on my mum's birthday in nineteen fifty-four and they stayed loyal, and true, until dad's death in two thousand and eight. At the moment he passed I was standing by his bed, mum was in an armchair in the corner of the room. She knew he had died and she said to me;

"Oh no what has he done now? Gone and left me? Well I am not going to let this stop me."

"Mum carried on for another four years. She outlived her younger sister; she had already survived a paralysing stroke, when she had been fifty years old. Most of her left side was useless for thirty years. She just got on with it as best she could. She could hobble about using the right side of her body to take her weight whilst swinging the rest of her form forward. She did not, could not, but absolutely, would not, use a stick, she hated the wheel chair. Following the stroke, she got fed up with the doctor and nurses, and told them that what had happened had happened, and she would get on with life the best she could, with what she had left. Stoic. If there is a gene for that it is from her I inherited it."

Doctor Samuels asked a question. "You are grateful for these two traits, I think?"

I responded: "Yes, yes I am. You mean insubordination and stoicism? shall I go on?" The doctor nodded. "In common with the majority of people, thankfully, I do not remember my conception, nor do I remember my birth. However, I can remember the birth of my brother. He was born thirty-five months after me. I can remember sometime before he was born. I remember my mum constructing maternity dresses and then feeding dresses, which had a zip from the collar to the midriff, so that when my brother arrived he would not go hungry, she had explained, although I did not really understand until after he was born. When he did arrive he came with a bit of umbilical cord protruding from his naval, it looked like a stick! The sun was pouring into dad and mum's bedroom, my brother was laying on the bed. On the table was breakfast orange juice in a glass jug, toast slotted in a chromium-plated toast rack. Butter and marmalade. Then the nurse came. So I have memories from the age of, I should say, two years nine months. I cannot be more precise, and I cannot put all the memories into chorological order. However, as I think, and speak, I am remembering even more, although I think not every detail, nor every minute. Some minutes seem to be lost or hidden. It seems to me now that time is different when one is a child. When one has not had such a lot of it the distance between Christmases is an eternity. Now I am more than sixty years old Christmas seems like five minutes ago, and actually these childhood moments are not so far away either.

Those early years of my life I spent a lot of time on my own. My parents were always about but they worked in the house where we lived, and they were always busy. I was not neglected, but people reading this, all these years later, would be truly amazed at my freedom, the lack of security, and the total absence of safety measures in my world. Seemly no thought that someone might wish harm on me. Of course in those days babies were left in prams outside shops, whilst mum just went in to get a pint of milk. It was the way things were, people did not have the anxiety produced by television and Internet, or a society that constantly pressured for defences against perceived threats and foes.

There were open coal fires in the grates, often with no fireguards. The immediate surrounds of the house were reasonably safe, not many cars, hardly a one, but a short walk across the grass and through the gate were the shops and a busy main road. One day I did venture beyond the gates and I rode my tricycle up the hill, past the shops, and the optician, and the garage, to where the road flattened out, diagonally across from the library. My dad must have noticed my absence, for I turned and looked about, and bought myself to the attention of several adults, who were concerned about my safety, when my dad came running up the hill and took me into his arms. I was not scolded, or admonished, no restrictions were placed upon my movements and things returned to normal."

"My parents ran a home for Working Girls, it was a hostel"

The doctor peered over his spectacles as if to ask for clarification on this terminology.

"I am not sure of that title in this day and age, however, it was a place where young women, who had just started working, or were just finishing with school, but for one reason or another, had had problems living at home, or elsewhere, could stay, so they came to live at Nut Tree House, on The Rose Tree Estate of children's homes. My dad and mum and their staff looked after these girls."

"Was this one of the places that has been in the news in the past couple of years?" Asked the doctor.

The doctor had his thumb under his chin, and his index finger on top of his chin, his fingers were curled, and he was squeezing his chin. I had read a bit of Desmond Morris so I was pretty sure that the doctor was evaluating what I had said. I continued;

"Yes, The Rose Tree Estate."

Doctor Samuels made a note of that and then he said;

"I see from the news that there is continuing controversy about that place."

"Well when you say that place it was a huge estate, seventy acres I think. There must have been forty large houses, and each had a lot of children in them. Yes I have seen the news. I was surprised to hear of all that, it really is not how I remember it. I cannot remember anything horrible happening to me." I Said.

Doctor Samuels said: "Well Kristopher please tell me all about it. Leave nothing out."

"At the entrance to the estate of homes was a Keeper's Lodge. Sometimes I would wander over there, and the Gate Keeper would allow me to sit on his highchair by his counter. He would give me paper and pencil to scribble with and he showed me how to draw a straight line using a round, black ruler, which, now I think about it, may have been the roller from an old typewriter. There was a blotting paper on the desk with a leather surround. People used to write with ink then, so most desks had a blotter for furniture."

"Well that is a detail." Said the doctor, with some joy in his voice.

"On the estate there was a black Labrador dog, he was called Rover, I am not sure who he belonged to. He and I were in a similar position, both left to roam. Sometimes he was there, when I say he, he could have been a she, I really had no idea, in fact I never thought about that until this minute. Rover and I would play until one of us got bored. He was not there all the time, but I suppose I was not always there when he was."

Doctor Samuels said. "I am truly interested in the details you are supplying; I am surprised that you can remember so much from so early in your childhood. I just have a query. Do you have a huge stack of photos or other things to remind you of all this? What I am trying to say is; are these really memories or have you seen photos and constructed these stories around them rather than these being your true experiences?"

I was surprised by the remarks, and the question, and I paused. Then I said;

"Well I did not have a camera, but I do have photographs of times before I can remember. They all seem to be studio portraits, and I really do not remember them being taken. There is one photograph of me sitting on the grass, to the front of Nut Tree House, who took it? I do not know. It is the only one I have and I do not remember the photograph being taken. Around the time my brother was born, dad and mum did buy a cine camera, and I have still some flickery movies from those. The strange thing is that the things I see on those films, of me, I do not remember. Certainly, they did not have a stills camera, and it was not cheap to run a cine camera. Film and processing were expensive. I am sure that when dad bought the film the price included the processing. They would not have been resources to waste inside a building with low light, and why would my dad take film in the Keeper's Lodge, for example? Besides there are so many things I can remember that no camera, cine, or otherwise, could have been anywhere near."

The doctor stopped squeezing his chin and gave a nod of his head as if to say, yes, ok you have convinced me.

"There was never any shortage of cardboard boxes, which I would make into train, and haul them behind my tricycle or my pedal car. My car was called Thunderbolt. One day I parked it in the television room, it was a big room, I should think 30 people could have sat in it. I parked my car too close to the open fire and when I returned the paint on the front offside wing had burnt away. That is funny I said offside as if it were a proper car with four seats, it only had room for me. I did not get burned. I tried to paint it over with my water paints and could not understand why the paint would not stick. At Christmas, someone gave me a painting-by-numbers set. There were many guests at a party that day, and I went off to get a cup of water, I crawled through a forest of legs, and into a quiet corner, in the gap between the sideboard and the wall. I dipped my brush into the water and then into one of the little paint pots, not knowing that it was oil paint. Now if I had worked out the differences between these two types of paint, maybe, I could have repaired my car. As it was I gave up on the painting-by-numbers because the paints would not work! It was quite a while before I received some tuition on the painting-by-numbers story. The results were unimpressive, but I was only around three years old at that point."

One other thing about Thunderbolt, the steering wheel was loose, it took a lot of effort to grip it in a way that would make the front wheels turn. That in its way they helped me to learn for I had to experiment to try and get around the problem. I can't say that I ever thought of asking dad to find a spanner and tighten up the nut so it gripped properly. I do remember him showing me how to change an electric plug. Green for earth, black for neutral red for live. Of course the colours have changed since then. I never forgot that lesson."

"Well, we will pick up there in two weeks time Kristopher." The doctor put down the clipboard and shook my hand. We went out into the reception; Doctor Samuels asked his secretary to type up the notes and transcribe the recording he had made and asked her to save them in the computer. I took my coat, hat and scarf from the hat stand. I put them on, I said goodbye to the receptionist and the doctor, and I went on my way.

Chapter 3
An Old Lady
Narrator

There was a song, from somewhere in the nineteen sixties. It was about a grand lady who had fallen on hard times. She was struggling to leave behind who she had once been. The song provokes the listener to have sympathy for The Grand Old Woman, who had lost her youth, and was now living in poorer circumstances. Pamela was, in her way, like the woman in the song. In the song there is a sailor who came over from France. A lifetime before, Pamela had fallen in love with a French Sailor. She had been only a girl then, just eighteen. A person had to be twenty-one years old to get the key to the door then, so she still had three years before she was, officially, an adult. She had left school when she was fifteen. Her home left her shortly afterwards when her father had killed her mother and was then hanged for his crime. Of course, it was very difficult for Pamela, but at least he, her father, could no longer 'bother' her, as she put it, coming to her bed in the night. Pamela found herself working in a laundry, the position provided lodgings, food and a bit of spending money.

Pamela met Marcel, and fell in love with this French Sailor, who was twenty years older than she. He would come and go from her life, as the tide and his ship would allow. Marcel did not love Pamela, but he was passionate about her, and because of her work position she was valuable to him.

She worked in the laundry of The Rose Tree Estate. She had a room to live in on the Estate, which gave Marcel access, not only to Pamela's charms, but also to a host of little boys and girls.

The pair had met when Marcel, had been in London. His ship travelled to many different destinations, carrying cargo of one sort or another, from one port to another. Like the sailor in song, Pamela's Sailor could dance and he could sing. Oh and how they danced, Bill Haley was 'Rocking around the Clock'. Pamela was thin then and Marcel could pick her up and throw her over his shoulder, up the right, up to the left, through the 'A' frame of his legs, they would jive the night away.

Marcel taught Pamela many things and when he was away she would practice them without him, in the hope that on his next visit, she could tell him about her adventures and make him pleased with her. There were many little ones to choose from, she used a mixture of bribery and threats to ensure that no victim would tell on her.

Then the French Sailor came no more, no explanation, no letter; there was actually was nowhere that he could have made a telephone call to. Why did he not write? Was he dead? Was he in prison? Did he not want Pamela anymore? Pamela waited and the loss harmed her.

*

Ten days after his last visit to Doctor Samuels, Kristopher had been into the town to do some shopping. He had to go to the bank; he needed some new white shirts and a pair of trousers. He found the shirts in one shop and the corduroy trousers in another. Then he needed some groceries, the nearest supermarket was near to the station, Kristopher was not a big fan of that supermarket but he did like the chocolate milk they sold, and he wanted to take a bottle of it home to drink whilst watching the television later that evening. It was a fine day, sun and blue sky with a few wispy clouds way up high.

Kristopher did not usually buy newspapers but as he was leaving the supermarket he passed the stand. The headline on one said 'The Witch of Rose Tree Estate?' There was a grainy black and white photograph of a woman on the cover of the papers, she was chubby and there was something about her. He picked up two copies, paid for them, and went out to his car. As he drove home, he was trying to grip the thought he had had when he saw the headline, but it eluded him.

Chapter 4
Session Two: Toy Cars
Kristopher

So here once again I was with Doctor Samuels. I found that I had grown in confidence, I had started to trust this kindly man, and I felt more open and more willing to tell him my stories.

"I had a massive collection of toy cars, my dad scratched my name on the bottom of every one. One day some of the boys from the other homes, on the estate, came to play. I was generous to a fault and gave each boy a couple of cars. My dad went and retrieved them all, that must have been difficult, but then, I suppose he had paid for them all. I had a teddy bear, and Jacko the monkey, a present from my grandparents. Jacko was so good he could hang on to a load of things and dangle mid air. One fine day I decided to wash all my cuddly toys. In those days such cuddly toys were filled with sawdust. It was all a bit messy, the dyes were not waterproof, and many of my toy companions had to live in the airing cupboard for a week to dry them out, my mum was worried that they would go mouldy.

There was a swimming pool on the estate. There was another pool in the town. The pool on the estate had no lifeguard when I was there. Although, apparently, there was someone employed to do that job. The girls had balls, hoops, and wooden rafts in the water. The pool in the town was full of people. On two occasions the girls took me swimming, and on both these occasions I ended up in the deep end, and both times I nearly drowned! It was frightening. I remember opening my eyes under the water, seeing the bubbles and the bottom of a raft. I pulled my arms against the water and somehow I survived. Instinct alone saved me, and I managed to climb out of the pool by the ladder. No one helped me. I do not think anyone noticed. Certainly nobody told my parents. Think of that doctor, I was around about four years of age when my parents put me in the care of some young women, who my parents were paid to care for. Young women who could not live in their own families, who actually had scant regard for my well-being. It is a wonder I survived my early years."

"Quiet extraordinary." Exclaimed the doctor. "Did that have any effect on you later in your life, were you afraid to go in the water, or to the swimming pool?"

"No, not at all, you could not keep me away from the water, I really loved it. I remember, much later, when I was in primary school, my friend David and I would go swimming every day of the summer holidays. We went to a different pool each day, then one day our bikes were stolen from outside one of the baths. We walked to the police station to report them stolen, and then walked home, we were probably nine years old at the time."

"After we lost our bikes we had to go by train, or bus, or walk. I remember a couple of times we got on the wrong train and ended up in places we really did not know. I suppose my parents must have funded these trips, so I suppose they must have thought they knew where I was, but really they had no idea at all. Having said that, they must have funded the swimming, it was me who earned the money for the bike. It cost eight pounds, second-hand. I earned the money by delivering leaflets through doors for an off-licence. There were a lot of leaflets. I am sorry doctor, I have strayed off the plot and into a different period of my life."

The doctor said. "Gosh, I have a feeling that if you put this in a book, people of my age, and younger, would not find it credible. Not many, if any, children are allowed to wonder far by themselves these days, but here I am watching, and listening, making notes, and recording all you say and it is quite clear that you are telling the absolute truth. Please Kristopher, continue."

"I wonder if that is because today's parents have less confidence in themselves. The other thing is that today there are so many stories of horrid things on the news. I am not sure there are any more 'bogie men' and women than there has always been. Of course my dad and mum had seen the Second World War so I suppose they saw the world through a different prism. Come to think about it my granny told me that she sent my mum and aunty of to school when the snow was so deep my aunty could hardly stand above it. My Granny said she said to my mum. 'You hold not tight to her hand, don't let it go or you might lose her in all this snow.'

I had freedom, Doctor Samuels, I am not sure if the world was more or less safe in the late nineteen fifties, but I am glad that those were my times, the cooped-up lives of today's mollycoddled youngsters would have driven my friends and I insane. None of my primary school pals, as far as I am aware, was ever molested, or kidnapped, or lost, or run over. We got bruises and cuts, and there were a lot of things that we would never have told our parents. Then there were things, out of our control, that did go wrong, my brother was bitten, on his bottom, by a, white Alsatian dog as he walked home alone from school. He was also standing by a wall, waiting to go into school, when a milk float crashed into the wall. It was the perimeter of a hotel; the wall was demolished at the gate entrance, bits of the brick and cement showered over him! It certainly was not just me who was so free, it was everybody I knew. Of course that was primary school, but as I have tried to indicate, even at three and four years old I was totally free. Nobody tried to fill my head with rules and danger; I could feel that fire was hot, when I was under the water I knew I had to get to the top. The only time I ever thought about eating a poisonous berry was in primary school, when a man came to talk to us about not eating berries, he gave a talk about trees, he said, the Yew-Tree was very toxic, and he showed us some red berries, he got a bit worked up, and forbade us to even touch them. Well I was very familiar with the tree. My pals and I hoped that, like Robin Hood, one day we would make a bow and arrow from a branch of it, there were two in the garden, yet I never went near those berries, nor did my pals. There were also apple trees, and cherry trees, and a huge old mulberry tree in that garden. All of us ate the apples, the cherries and the mulberries but none of us thought of eating the poisonous berries, until this, so-called; expert put the idea in our heads. When you think of the two and a half million years women and men have wondered about the Earth, it seems that quiet a few of them, like my pals and me, did not eat them either. As for mushrooms and toadstools, I can't think that any of my pals ever wanted to try eating them. I do know some people eat the wrong things, I am not meaning to be flippant, I am just saying how my life was. I will say again, I am glad that's was. I do remember being told not to take sweets from a stranger, and never to get into the car of a stranger. I also remember one snowy day when my friend Paul and I were walking by the common, near cinder pitches. We used to play football on the cinders from the furnaces, you never wanted to fall on that stuff, boy you would rip your knees and be grazed if you did. A car did pull up and a woman called out to us and asked us if she could give us a lift in her car. We, in unison, shouted 'No!' and ran off over the common."

"So Kristopher, the same time Tuesday week?" Asked the doctor. I agreed and left for home.

*

"I have some cine-film, I tried to video all my dad's old films, he had tried to edit things together, in those days he had to splice the film and stick it together with glue. It was a difficult process. I do not want to criticise but the order of the editing often left much to be desired. There is one small clip of his old black car. I searched the Internet for pictures; there were many cars, from the nineteen forties and nineteen fifties that looked similar. I tried to pin it down from the badge, the film is blurred, my best guess is that it is the Vauxhall badge but I could not find a picture to exactly match the video."...... When Tuesday week arrived I plunged straight into the session with stories about dad's car.....

Chapter 5
Jason's Leap
Narrator

Jason could not say what the worst experience he had had was. In contrast to Kristopher, babbling on about his life, Jason had no parents that he remembered. His first memories were, he recalled, of a loud, fat, shouty, woman who slapped him on the soft part of his leg, behind his right knee. He had never felt such a physical sting before and it alerted his brain to the idea of pain. It made him ever afraid that there could be even worse pain somewhere. The worst of it; he had not expected this pain from that direction. It left a scar somewhere, deep inside him; that he should always be on the alert for loud, fat, shouty, women with big hands, and who moved fast. What he had done to deserve the punishment? He had no idea. He cried and he grizzled and two streams of mucus flowed from his dear little nose, and as no one offered a handkerchief, or tissue, he was forced to try to catch the stream with his tongue.

Jason had many such memories. So many nights, actually every night of his childhood they put him in bed, in the dormitory he shared with five others. He would whimper until the woman with the spoon arrived. The liquid she gave him tasted awful but then he was asleep until morning. When someone would shout because, he, Jason, had wet the bed. It seemed, looking back, that very few, if any, of the people, who were supposed to care for him, had the faintest idea of what it was like to be a tiny human. To a tiny human the world is full of shouty giants. From whom all Jason felt was anger, and not one ounce of love, compassion, or kindness.

It would be wrong to take this, one sided, emotional view of Jason's, as a simple statement of fact. Indeed, many of the carers, encountered by Jason in his early years, were kind and caring people. However, Jason's memory of them was overshadowed by the brutality of the others.

Jason spent the whole of his childhood on The Rose Tree Estate. There were several years when his school provided a haven; he had the same teacher during those years a good woman with a round face and kind eyes. She could see the hurt in Jason and, although there were thirty-seven other children in her class, Miss. Tomkins did her best to make Jason's school days into a good experience. Jason responded well to this, he felt secure in the classroom and dreaded the end of each day when he had to return to Rose Tree.

Once grown, Jason tried to make a go of life away from Rose Tree. By a stoke of luck he found employment as a lorry driver for a department store, taking goods to people's houses. He worked alone and was trusted. He lived in a shared house with some fairly nice people, and for about five years, things went very well, especially when you consider the circumstances of Jason's start in life.

Then Jason met a girl, and she liked him, the feeling was mutual, and, after about a year, Serena asked him why he never seemed to want to touch her, or kiss and cuddle. He told her that he did not know how. So Serena started to try and teach him. You might think that would have been an easy thing to do. Far from it, you cannot give what you do not possess, and intimacy is both give and take. Yes he got the hang of the cuddles and the kisses, but Jason could not find the love element which glues it all together. Yes I know people have sex without love; if that is your thought you have missed the point.

It was that night when Serena suggested she might stay over, that was when it all came to a head. She thought Jason would cope and Jason wanted to. Serena was so pretty, her skin was soft and it radiated warmth. She took the lead and unbuttoned Jason's shirt. Then she unbuttoned her dress. Her chestnut coloured hair flowed over her shoulders and she kissed him gently, with tenderness. Jason was so fortunate that all this was happening with someone so full of love as Serena. Someone who could feel the pain he carried. Then they stood naked looking at each other and Jason's face was asking the question what do we do now? Although he said not one word. Serena lay on his single bed and pulled him to her, but then calamity was upon them. For it was in this warm, and tender moment, when all should have been right with the world, the first time making love to a beautiful young woman who cared so deeply for him, that those deep, and hidden, memories erupted and spewed all over the tranquil scene. He shook and he shuddered, and sweat came all over his body. He panted for air and Serena thought that he had been taken ill. He pulled away from her and grappled with his clothes, she looked in disbelief, she could not make it out. What was wrong with her? What had she done to cause this? In a moment Jason was gone. Out of the room, down the stairs and into the cold February night with only his jacket for warmth. Serena did not know what had happened. In those days there were few telephones. She felt alone, empty and hollow. She dressed and followed Jason's path, down the stairs, and into the cold February night, she had on her warm winter coat, scarf and gloves. As she made her way through the street-lamped town she felt a flake of snow on her face. She arrived at the bus stop and had to wait. She wondered where Jason had gone, she felt dirty, and silly, and betrayed.

It took Jason a good hour to climb the road, up hill all the way. He had never been to the spot before, but he knew all about it, it was often in the news. He walked past the telephone post, he could see the plaque and he had a notion of what was written on it. It would had made no impression if he had stopped to read it, for in his mind he could feel the hot, unpleasant-smelling breath, of the loud, fat, shouty, woman who had slapped him, when he had been so small. Being naked with Serena is what bought it all back.

You remember about half of what you hear, unless you get the right stimulation to remember more. The only time in his life he had been naked with a woman, before this day, was back then. He had no memory of it until Serena tried to pull him down on top of her. In the glorious moment, when Jason could have felt the power of real love from Serena, in his mind he found himself in the arms of the loud, fat, shouty woman and she had wiped the mucus from his nose and undressed herself, then she had undressed Jason. She had pulled is naked little form onto her great whale of a stomach, she had rubbed his body up and down her body using his tiny foot, pushing it into wet and warm places until she had shuddered. It was at that moment that Jason stepped of the edge; his body flew through the cold, dark February night. His bones cracked on the rocks below and a huge smashing, crashing, wave ripped up his corpse and dragged it into the sea.

Serena really never got over the experience. Every time she came to make love with a hansom young man. She felt that they might rip away from her, as had Jason. Of course they did not, for none of them had been bought up on The Rose Tree Estate.

Chapter 6
Session Three: Freedom
Kristopher

"My dad's car was a source of some distraction. It was always parked out at the back of the big house. It was easy to slip into the car, handle was at the front of the door, and the slight incline meant that the door swung back, as it was hinged at the mid column, the doors opened the other way from that which is now the norm. Sitting at the steering wheel and, in imagination, I could drive off down the road. The estate was private, there were very few cars that passed down the roads, on occasion my dad would sit me on his lap and let me steer as he drove. It was a black car, there were many makers with similar looking vehicles, all came in black, with round headlights and leather seats. I think I said something like that to you before in one of our previous sessions. To indicate which direction it was to turn there were two, amber coloured, arms, like arrows, which would pop out from the mid column between the front and back doors. To start it required a starting handle. Cold and damp days were troublesome when it came to getting the thing going. So dad would open the bonnet at night, and put a blanket over the engine to try and keep out the frost. I am not sure to what extent that worked but I do recall, many times, seeing one side of the bonnet open, the bonnet opened along the length, rather than the width of the car and was in two parts. My dad, with greasy, back oil-covered hands, tried to dry out the distributor cap. One, rainy day we went on a journey in the car, and smoke and flames appeared from beneath the bonnet. My dad had to stop the car and the fire brigade had to come, the road on which we were was blocked, my dad had forgotten to remove the blanket before we started our journey! I never thought of this before but I wonder if he got into trouble for that? I think that that was the end of that old car. Sometime after this my dad bought a new car, another in black and so proud he was of it, it was a totally different beast, kind of light and fun.

On a great many, tedious, occasions I had to tag along with my dad whilst he went about his business, visiting parents of the girls he cared for. We would drive all over London he would park and leave me in the car, for hours, it seemed to me, with not very much to do. On one of these visits, in front of one girl's homes, and her mother, I said;

"This is not a very nice place."

It was an innocent statement, from a tiny boy, but I got a good telling off for that.

Dr Samuels made his first intervention of the session;

"I think it does seem somewhat sharp to me. Leaving you alone in the car. I have a boy, who is just coming up four now. I would not leave him in the car, apart from any other dangers; the wrath of my wife would be something to fear. I am also interested that at such a tender age you were able to make a statement, and understand that it caused displeasure. I can see how the world in which you grew up was so completely different from the early nineteen eighties, when I was a similar age, and how radically changed things are now. My four year old is always in sight, always protected, there are annoying plastic covers in the electric sockets, things that stop cupboards opening, gates on the stairs, there is no way that my wife would allow a coal fire, just in case someone got burned."

I continued: "Well this is a bit out of sync from this part of the story but I was six years old when my sister was born. Mum went into a small hospital to have the baby, but there were complications and she was taken to the big hospital. She was in the hospital for a good few days. Each evening I would go with my dad to visit mum, where my younger brother was I do not know. When we got to the small hospital I was not allowed to go in covered in all my germs, it was apparently OK for dad to take all his germs in with him. I was just left in the street. Oh how boring it was! This small hospital was in a residential street and the only building to break that monotony was a chemist shop. That had little to capture the imagination except for two very large glass bottles which were in the window, one filled with blue liquid and one filled with red. I must have had to kick my heels for a good half an hour each visit. Totally alone on a street, just around the corner was a busy main road. I was happy when they took mum to the big hospital. I was not told why, of course, but these visits were far better for me. It was a busy street with loads of people. It was a very busy main road with cars, lorries, and buses. Across the street was a large common but a little way up from the hospital was a toyshop. It had a great window display. Cars, trains, balls, hula-hoops, balsa wood planes. I could go on. After these visits dad would take me to the café across the road. There was a bar, we sat on stools and they had milk shakes. The thing is I was safe enough on my own at six years old, I could make a joke here, Dr. Samuels, and tell you that three years later when my youngest brother was born, I had my own apartment and I was driving an Italian sports car with a name that rhymes with *bikini*, brand new in nineteen sixty-three, but I won't! I will tell you at the age of nine I would never have dreamed of going with dad to wait outside the hospital, by that time I really had my own things to be getting along with. Yes, the world of today is certainly much more risk averse, I am not sure if that makes us safer, I actually think it makes us less self-reliant, after all, I was drowning in the pool, nobody had given me swimming lessons, so something inside my own head made me do what I did, and I lived!"

Doctor Samuels said: "We still have a few minutes please continue with your stories."

"Well, if there were visits at night, there would surely be a Fish and Chip shop, somewhere close by. The smell of the frying fat would waft down the streets, in those days, and I would often ask for two-penny-worth of chips, I did not often get them, but I always asked.

It was my dad's presence that I felt most of in these times. He took me to the garage when the car needed servicing. I was curious to know what it might be like to sit in the car whilst the car was elevated on the pneumatic ramp so the mechanic could see underneath the car. So they let me climb in and I was transported high above the garage floor. I cannot say that I enjoyed it for I demanded, in no uncertain terms, that the car should be lowered so I could disembark.

When my dad got his new car we had to travel to the garage, to the main dealers, for the servicing. We drove it there and got the bus back home and then a day or two later we took the bus back to collect it, we disembarked at the Sweet Loaf pub to collect the Anglia. Not far from there my mum had embarked on a course at the College, over the years she trained to be a *Cordon Bleu Chef*, and a teacher of cooking. My dad and I would sometimes meet her and then we would drive her home.

Drives in those days were different from now. There were fewer cars about, however, that did not save one from traffic jams. Some of those in the nastiest places. You may know that gas can be made from coal. There was a gas works and I remember holding my breath, until I nearly burst, whilst stuck in traffic at this spot. The smell was terrible, gagging and eye watering. Other times we would go to the country, white coloured roads and a country garage where a mechanic put down his spanner, and wandered over, whilst rubbing his hands on an old dirty rag before putting petrol into dad's car.

The local town often featured in my young life. Visits to do shopping, on the bus, were frequent. *Barrett's*, a big department store was a great place to go, for there were often real ponies to ride, and there was a pretend space ship to fly, insert a penny and off to the moon. There was also the fruit and vegetable market, which even I - at so young a time in my life - loved. The men in their flat caps and the women in head scarves and wide skirts. The stallholders shouting out, whatever they shouted.

It is not possible for me to put these memories into chronological order, but these memories are vivid and they are copious."

"Kristopher I am afraid that I must stop you, I do wish you could carry on, you were really on a roll. However, I have other responsibilities, I will look forward to seeing you in a fortnight." The doctor stood up and showed me to the door.

*

I was sorry that the session was over too. My brain had really caught the idea and was throwing up many memories which had not appeared to me since the events had occurred.

Chapter 7
Willow
Narrator

Grace lived in a bed-sitting room, above a kebab shop. It was OK, but the area was noisy twenty four hours, seven days a week. If she could have gone somewhere better, she would have, but she had not the means, nor the knowledge, to extract herself from this place. Indeed, although this place was no palace, she knew that palaces are relative to where you have lived before, and this was better than the commune squat she had come from. It was the only bed-sitting room in the building. Although it was small, she had nobody to share the bathroom with, and that made it, for her, better than the palace of the former president of the United Arab Emirates and ruler of Abu Dhabi. Grace had cut a photograph of his palace from a magazine, which she had found in her dentist's waiting room, she did ask if she could take it. She stuck it to her wall with toothpaste, dreaming of a day when she might visit and actually see it.

Grace had been born in the mid nineteen seventies, she was not entirely sure of her actual birth date. Her parents had been heavily into drugs when she was born and no one knew of her existence before both her parents were murdered. The police found her in the room with the dead bodies. No one knew how many days she had been alone since they had died, or indeed, how she had survived. She was a survivor. She was obviously very hungry when she was found, and her little body was covered in scabies, they were crusted.

So the first home that Grace had, after the horrendous start in life was Willow House on The Rose Tree Estate. She was one of forty babies and infants who were shepherded by many young women who had the title Nursery Nurse. A number were still pursuing their NNEB qualification (National Nursery Examination Board). The house was divided into four sections, with ten children in each. The groups would intermingle. The reason for this was to ensure that groups were not overwhelming, that each child was well cared for, and that their needs were met. Each section had a play area, dining area, and a sluice with toilets. The children had bedrooms on the second floor. There was no television or radio. The staff, the Nursery Nurses, were there each day from seven in the morning, until seven in the evening. They took it in turns to have a couple free hours in the day. So the children were supervised the whole day long. The night staff arrived spot on seven o'clock. The other employees were kitchen staff, a gardener, and a maintenance man; this great big family was overseen by a kindly matron, Mrs. Jefferson, who lived, with her family, in a separate house behind Willow House. Some of the other members of staff had rooms within the house, whereas some lived off the estate and travelled in daily.

Willow House was a grand place. Indeed the whole estate was beautiful. There was a lot of grass and many mature trees. The grounds were well maintained, as were all the buildings, fences, roads and pavements. A couple of hundred years before the land had been a farm. Now it was seventy acres, with about forty large homes for children and young people. There was a laundry, a swimming pool, and a school. Each of the houses were run autonomously, but there were contacts between children and staff of all the homes; and at various times of the year, there were events and activities which bought all the members of The Rose Tree Estate together. At Christmas all would gather around the Crib, at the entrance to the estate, they would sing carols under the big monkey-puzzle tree, bedecked in coloured lamps. At Easter there was a huge Easter Egg Hunt, and an Easter Bonnet Parade. In the summer there was a sports day and at the beginning of the autumn there was a brass band concert. Each house on the estate catered for different ages of children.

For many of the estate's residents there was a progression from one house to another, as they lived their whole childhood at Rose Tree. Some of the children were adopted, whilst some went back to live with their natural parents. Others grew up, and then left to live their lives as adults.

The daily routine at Willow House began with dressing. Those who thought they were big enough would put their own clothes on, babies had their nappies changed, and anyone who needed help, got it. Then it was down the stairs for breakfast. Hands washed in the sluice room sink. There were high chairs for some, ordinary chairs for others. Cereal, toast, butter and marmalade were available, and, on Sunday, boiled eggs. Next each young person would drink a cup of milk, followed by hand washing, mouth wiping, medicine for those who required it, toilet and nappy changes, for any who was in need. The toilet words were 'wee' and 'motion'.

Once all this was done it was playtime. Depending on the weather, that would be inside or outside in the garden. The garden was really lovely with grass lawns, flower borders, trees and a smooth tarmac path which divided the lawn and provided a good road for tricycles and scooters. The play was supervised by the nursery nurses. They joined in sometimes, and watched at other times. Half way through the morning it was a drink and biscuit time. Then, all to soon, it was lunchtime. Washing hands, sitting at the table, bibs, reminders of manners, elbows off the table. Then the trolley would arrive with plates and whatever the cook had prepared that day. After lunch it was nap time. Not everybody napped of course. Then it would be story time, followed by some other excitement. In the summer they went for trips up to the woods, or to the park. If it was hot there might have been a water pistol fight in the garden. No one had time to be bored. After tea came the challenging part of the day; for the nursery nurses had to finish at seven, and the night staff wanted to arrive when the children were tucked up in bed. So to get everyone bathed and in pyjamas in time was a real stretch. The stretch often had the effect of exciting the children, and of course, that led the nursery nurses into a few battles with their charges.

It was at these moments that the system faltered, for the children, despite the bravado of their day, were really only babies. The best place for babies is with parents who love them. Now these babies were shown affection, they were cuddled and they were certainly cared for, but children do not have on/off switches, and none of the nursery nurses had had children of their own. Really, until a person is a parent, it is impossible to know what it is like. Parents do not clock off at seven in the evening, not to reappear until seven in the morning. Parents, by and large, do not take two days of a week, two days is a long time in a baby's life.

It may be quiet impossible, unless you have been a child in such circumstances, to really appreciate the horrors some of these little people experienced before they came to Willow House. Drugged-up abusive parents. Real hunger. Some arrived in police cars, they were found wandering the train station dressed only in rubber pants. Unbelievably, some of these poor mites had had violence done upon them, hits, punches and even cigarettes stubbed out on their tiny bare arms. Some had lost their parents in accidents. Some had been fostered out or even adopted, but things did not work out. So here they all were, a bundle of damaged humanity being cared for by loving, well meaning, well trained, young women. Many of the young women having come from troubled backgrounds themselves, most of them lacking in worldly experience, and most lacking the deep inner confidence which fills those about them with security. It was not anybody's fault, everyone was doing their best within the system that they had. Much of what was done was wonderful. Some of what was done would, no doubt, have left huge scars on the children, and would be seen as wrong, especially looking back through a prism of forty years.

The challenge of getting all to sleep before the night staff arrived was often achieved by dosing the children with *Oblivon*. One spoonful was enough to secure sleep in the most excited little boy, at one moment jumping up and down on the bed, and the next, unconscious beneath the blankets. At the other end of the sleep, the knock-on effect was, sometimes, wet beds. Although wet beds were also caused by anxiety, or too much to drink, and too deep a sleep. Wet beds often caused friction. Sometimes an astonished pair of watery eyes would gaze up at an angry adult face wondering why the person who owned it was shouting at them; after all they had just been sleeping. Children do not consciously 'wet the bed' but they are conscious when they are told off for it.

Something that was unknown, in the nineteen seventies, when Grace became a part of this Rose Tree Estate organisation, was the psychology of such tiny people. When people are little, the whole world, as far as they are concerned, exists to serve them. Often people make derogatory remarks about 'ego' but ego is an essential part of the human survival mechanism. Most people mature and understand that they are not the centre of the universe by they time they attain adulthood.

You might use this as a metaphor; The Greek, Claudius Ptolemy (cAD 100-c170), mathematician and astronomer worked out that the Earth is a sphere. By 1493, the German, Martin Behaim constructed the first globe. 1543, the Polish astronomer Copernicus, published *De revolutionsibus orbium coelestium*, 'The Revolutions of Heavenly Spheres' With this work he showed that Ptolemy was right about the spherical nature of the planet we live on, but that it was not the centre point of the universe, neither was the sun the centre of the universe, but the sun is the centre of this part of the universe. So the egotistical people, who inhabited the earth cAD100 grew up, and a thousand and four hundred years later, the occupants of planet Earth were given the message that they are not the centre of everything. Not everyone got the message, even when Apollo 8 went to the moon, in nineteen sixty-eight, some folk still believed that the Earth is flat.

That is how it works in individuals too. At the beginning we are the centre of our universe, by the time we are grown we realise that we are not. It takes time to grow up, and not everyone gets the message.

Sometime, around the time that Grace arrived in Willow House, June, a twenty-one-year-old, Nursery Nurse, realised that if she sat down on the floor whilst one of her infant charges stood beside her she could see the world more from the child's angle. June may not have been the first to note this simple idea, but she was a person who took it seriously and used it. She realised the child could look her straight in the eye. No more squinting up at a giant, no more staring straight at a knee or thigh. June went on to be the matron of a children's home. She studied child psychology, and later she wrote books about caring for children. They should have been sold in the supermarket and have been at the top of the bestseller lists. Sadly they were treated as academic theses, and collected dust on library shelves instead of making June wealthy. That was sad for her and the many children who could have benefited from the empathy which surged through all her blood vessels.

June said to one of her colleagues: "Have you ever stopped and looked into the eyes of these children who are in our care? We are not their parents, they know that. How would you feel if you no longer had your parents? It is all in their little wide eyes. They want to trust you but sometimes they are not sure, but then there is no one else, so they have to trust you anyway."

Tiny people see their world from where they are, they are the centre, so whatever happens, good, or bad, it must have been them that caused it. That is what makes little humans so vulnerable and that is the very reason that so many adults find life more difficult than it need be, for early wounds are so much deeper than adult wounds. If you think about it, babies have less physical and mental abilities to absorb the shocks. Try to and imagine yourself in this situation... The woman you have known as mum, for two and a half years, has your naked, tiny, body wrapped in a blanket, you are wearing only a pair of rubber pants because your mum could not wash the only *Terries* cloth nappy she could afford to buy for you. The year is nineteen seventy-two. Your mother still has not got through the depressions she suffered after your birth. Your father disappeared shortly after your conception, and your mother has no family about her, for they disowned her when she took up with your father. Your mother tried her hardest, but lack of funds lack of support has finally got the better of her. The thumping in her skull will not go away, and every day it gets louder. She has reached the end of the line. So she has wrapped you in a blanket, with your rubber pants, for she thinks that if they find you alone, the authorities will have to care for you, better than they care for the pair of you. She sits you on the wooden bench in the underground station. The air is thick and it is always warm, too warm, in the underground, so you, her precious little child, will not be cold. She looks up to the lighted display and she feels the air move, wind like, that she knows precedes the arrival of the red dragon, which is the underground train. She hears the noise, and so do you, but you have heard it before, and mum is with you, so the dragon will not frighten you. The noise grows louder, the wind grows stronger, your mother kisses your head. The people on the platform shuffle, and suddenly your mother is gone. People are in the way, you cannot see, and there is a scream from the crowd. You don't know what has happened but you know your mum has gone and she will not be back. Time stands still and you remember nothing of what happened next, but suddenly you are in a car with a woman who wears a uniform and a hat. You are driving along in a car, you never did that before. You cry, and the tears are a flood. You want your mum. Suddenly you are at the door. The great big green door of a huge house, the door opens and the uniformed woman turns to go and a stranger picks you up. The only good fortune you have at this moment is that it is June, and June already worked out what it might be to be lost and alone and to be two and a half years old and dressed only in rubber pants.

Chapter 8
Session Four: In the Psychiatrists Chair
Kristopher

"So we are already eight weeks into this Kristopher." Said the kindly Doctor Samuels. I re-read the transcripts and my notes from our first three sessions. I think soon we will be coming to the heart of the matter. So thank you for all of what you have said, and if you are willing to continue, I am looking forward to hearing more of your stories. Are you comfortable to carry on?"

I was back in the comfy leather chair, and in this quiet, safe space. I thought the only thing that is missing here is a grand-father clock, and its comforting tick and tock. Of course that would have been a complete distraction. I did think though that given half the chance Doctor Samuels would have accommodated one. I felt sure he must be a great fan of such items, I made a note to ask him, but I decided to wait until his work with me had ended.

"Yes doctor, I am happy, and eager, to continue. I think we had just been on a tour of the shops when we had to finish the last session." I said. "I did a bit more searching for my dad's car, I have a little bit of film of it. I think my mum took the film of him in the car and he must have taken the bit where she was standing by the car. He was smartly dressed and two of the girls they looked after were also smartly dressed in the back. A black girl and another who was a white girl with blond hair. The film shows both the front and the back ends of the car; I am sure it was a Morris Twelve. I think it had indicators rather than those amber stick things that showed which direction the driver was about to go. So why am I telling you this? Well just so that you know - although I do remember many things clearly, I suppose I do not remember everything perfectly."

Doctor Samuels replied. "Nobody does. You, Kristopher do have an exceptional recollection, there are few with such capacity. The thing about our brains is this; we record everything we see, touch, smell and feel. There is not time to relay, or remember all we do. Obviously, it would take as much to tell another person everything we have done, as it took us to do it. Then it would take a bit longer for all the things surrounding the event would also have to be described. The room; the open space; the other people that were there; was it night or day; hot or cold; what was the weather; were you feeling well; were you happy; were the other people involved sad? etc. etc. etc. So your brain records everything, and given the right stimulation, you could recall it all. So you look up the car and find a picture and it helps tease out things that are hidden away in the corners of your brain. Of course that is what these sessions are all about. Finding out what we have hidden away.

The thing is when you are telling me your stories, you cannot give every detail, so your brain dips into the recorded data and pulls out the highlights, or the low lights, and you tell me of those. Generally when we relay stories we tell the peaks and the end, we edit out the rest because there is not time to relay it all. I will just say something more about this. You have a system in your brain, some call it the Reticular Activating System, it was a man called Otto Deiters who devised the name and the theory behind it. Sadly he died in eighteen sixty-three of typhoid fever. It has much to do with being asleep and being awake and it also allows people to filter out things that are going on around about so it is possible to concentrate on a particular issue. For example, there are people who may have to go to live near to an airport. When they first arrive the noise is all but unbearable. After three weeks, it takes three weeks to form a new habit, the noise of the aeroplanes becomes just something that is there in the background and it no longer disturbs. You have a sceptical frown on your forehead Kristopher!" The doctor smiled.

"I hope you may have a deeper understanding of what these sessions are about now Kristopher. Our brains are much like computers; they collect up all the information from our environment and store it in files. Some files we lock away because we do not like what is contained in them. You know people often think that we only communicate with words, but most communication is via feelings. They say 'go with your gut', and often that is right. For hundreds of thousands of years those gut feelings have served our species very well, a lot of the time."

Doctor Samuels ruffled the papers on his aluminium clipboard, his gold pen glinted and he said. "Why yes, you do have a sharp memory Kristopher."

I said. "I think I do but there are things that get tucked away, I can see you are right. So back to The Rose Tree Estate. If I were to go out of the gate, by the gatehouse, and turn left there was a sweet shop, it was a light airy place and there were two large windows, with displays of wonderful goodies. Do you remember that great children's book *'The Giraffe, The Pelican and Me'*? Oh no sorry I got that wrong *'The Giraffe, The Pelly and Me.'*? *Roald Dahl* features a 'Grubber', an old fashioned sweet shop. That was what this place was, but it was also elegant. The Sugar Mice were captured under a shiny glass dome which rested on a white round platter. The glass jars of boiled sweets were in absolutely regimented lines on the shelves behind the counter. There was coconut ice, fudge and nougat behind glass in the cabinet which formed part of the counter. Sorry, I am maybe providing a little too much detail here." I apologised.

"Absolutely not, the more detail the better." was the doctor's response.

"If I were to go out of the gate and cross the road, there was another sweet shop. It was the opposite, dark and cramped. I did not like it so much but they sold something the other shop did not have, I do not know what they were called, I did not know then and I do not know now. They had some small plastic tubes, which were sold with a small plastic spoon. Inside the tube as a paste. The paste was in bands of different colours. If you ever visited the Isle of Wight and went to Alum Bay you could fill a test tube with different coloured sands, it looked like one such test tube. Each of the colours tasted different from the others, and by the time the tube was almost empty the plastic spoon was only just long enough to extract the best of the flavours -- the bottom one. Oh how I struggled to get to the flavour. To this day I have no idea what the flavour was, it tasted of itself, I could not say it tasted like this or that -- No."

In my mind I could see clearly all that I was describing to the patiently listening doctor. In my mind I crossed back over the road, when the traffic light turned red and stopped the cars from moving. I had my white paper bag of sweeties grasped tightly in my hand. There was the red telephone box with the old, black-painted metal and Bakelite phone. You could push your money into the slot and press button A when the call was answered, or retrieve your coin with button B. I crossed the lawn, to the front of the house and sat beneath the Monkey Puzzle Tree. I had my Little Boy Blue, shorts, and stripy tee-shirt, and hat on with my blue sandals. It was warm summer time. I ate all the sweeties up. I am glad I was a child then, un-hounded by the sugar fearists of modern times. I was not fat and I brushed my teeth. I never understood all the stuff about *'Milky Way the sweet you can eat between meals without ruining your appetite'* -- even after a big bag of sweets I could still eat my dinner.

Doctor Samuels coughed.

"Is everything alright Kristopher? You have not said anything for a couple of minutes."

"Oh I am sorry, I was thinking." Then I had to tell Doctor Samuels all of what was in the previous paragraph.

"Do you know crisps used to be just plain? I wonder if that original crisp company is still in business? I don't know. I do not think there were any flavours back then, if you opened a packet inside the bag you found the crisps and in amongst them were dark blue twists of waxed paper, inside the twist was salt, which you could then pour over your crisps. If you liked a lot that was fine if you did not like salt your did not have to pour it on."

The doctor was surprised.

"No, I did not know that, it sounds like a good idea, maybe they should bring it back. Now we have caught up. Please carry on."

I cleared my throat and took a sip of water from the glass on the table in front of the leather chair.

"In one room of the big house, it was a big room, there was a toilet, right in the middle with a fence around three sides and a gate to the front. The fence and gate were made of plywood on a frame and painted. Only about a meter high, it was not much protection for a user's modesty. This toilet was never actually used, as far as I know. The room had two doors, one into the house and the other out into the grounds at the back of the house. The room was full of bicycles. The only space was where the toilet stood and the path between the two doors and a great big white enamelled sink. I do not recall anyone riding any of the numerous bikes, and to whom they all belonged I never knew. What had this strange room been used for before my parents took over this home?

The girls, whom, my dad and mum cared for were all fine to me. I have vivid memories of many of their faces, some names, and their clothes. The dresses which dropped into gaily coloured skirts. Their faces were all different colours. I remember them dancing to rock and roll records on the lawn in the front of the house. Driving with them in my dad's car to their work, or interviews, or to the shops. Sometimes they would be dressed-up smart, and sometimes more casual. I remember snowy days, throwing snowballs and running and sliding on an icy strip they had created. I remember walks into the woods on the common. Someone pointing out the clay soil and telling me that was the stuff to make pots out of. I remember going with my mum and some of the girls to The Trooping of the Colour in London. We saw the Queen".

"Alright Kristopher, that was very good, I am sorry we have to finish it there today, but can I ask you, have you been to The Rose Tree Estate recently?"

"No I have not, not since we left there when I was four years old."

"I wondered if you and I might make a pilgrimage there together instead of you coming here for your next session. It will take most of the day but I think it will be well worth it." He enthused.

I hesitated. For it crossed my mind that maybe none of what I had said was true in the physical world, what if we went there and there was no trace of all the things I had spoken of. After sixty years would, or could, there be anything left? If there was anything, would it obliterate all these precious memories that I have been relating?

I said: "I would like to think about that before I say yes, can I call you in a day or two?"

"Surely you can." He said.

I queried: "I mean what good would that do? I am very fond of the memories I have, I am not sure I want to disillusion myself."

He responded: "Of course that is possible, but I think it might also be that a visit would unlock more, and maybe we might find ourselves in the roots of whatever it is that your brain is hiding from you."

I felt a sheen of sweat on my brow and a shivered slightly at the prospect of having to confront whatever it was - for whatever it was I knew that he was right. I was hiding from it because I was scared. No, I am misleading you, I was petrified of it, but I really did not know what it was."

Chapter 9
A Whirlpool of Problems.
Narrator

As in every area of life, both good, and bad, are a part of the equation, whatever it is. Some parents are good, some parents are bad, some people are good at their job, some people are not. There are those people who may be irredeemable, but for the most part, people try hard, and give what they can, in whatever endeavour they pursue. A person may be good or bad, but of course, the situation in which they perform will have a bearing. If a person is in the army and they fail to make their bed correctly they could receive a heavy penalty, if they stay a night in a hotel and they do not make the bed there is no penalty. Many people are quick to judge other people, after all, it is easier to see the faults in others than the faults in oneself. It is very difficult to be critical of yourself. You know what you know, and you do what you do, and you feel about yourself as you feel. So, when there is crime do you brae and shout for revenge, or wonder exactly why, whatever happened -- *happened?* Is it possible to have empathy? I will leave you to answer that question for yourself. I will say this; if you were in the other person's shoes what would you have done? Could you have controlled yourself?

There are two motivators in humans, one is desire and the second is fear. These are internal forces. Some people think that they can manipulate other people by using these tools, and, to certain degree, that is possible. If a person uses these tools for themselves, as an internal mechanism, desire can take them to their dream with pinpoint accuracy. If internalised fear is their motivation the consequences, to others and themselves, are unpredictable and can be devastating.

Everyone who reads this will have at some time been criticised. If the person who criticised was wise they would have said something like:

"Oh yes, I see what you have done, shall I tell you how I did the same thing?" Pause for a positive reply... Continue... "This is how I managed it. It may be worth a try. You might get a better result."

Using that technique the critic gets permission to offer advice, and then offers an alternative to what has been done, without any claim of superiority. The only real way to criticise is to get a person's permission first. For example, "If I knew something about what you have done, that you probably would not like to hear, would you want me to tell you about it?" Now the person might say yes they might say no. If they say no it may not be long before they change their mind and ask you to repeat your earlier reflections. When someone asks you for information they are ready to hear it.

Sadly most people who criticise do not know that technique. So instead of helping people to get better, criticism usually damages, and often destroys, the self-confidence of people. Sometimes to the extent that they spend most of their time in defence mode with their shields up. That can manifest in a withdrawal from society, or aggression, on a sliding scale, depending on the damage.

So imagine yourself as a two-and-a-half-year-old stranded on an underground station, your mummy just left you. Maybe not consciously, but deep down inside, you wonder what you did to cause that -- and if your mummy does not want you anymore, *How do you feel about that for criticism?!*

All of the girls and boys who arrived at the houses on The Rose Tree Estate had been damaged before they arrived, some to the extent that repairs might never be possible. Sadly, once at Rose Tree, they were at further risk of damage, for they had now entered a great pool of humanity all swirling and whirling about in damage.

It is written that Plato said that the young should be surrounded by fair works, sounds, and beauty.

(Amid fair sights and sounds, and receive the good in everything; and beauty, the effluence of fair works, shall flow into the eye and ear, like a health giving breeze from a purer region, and insensibly draw the soul from earliest years into likeness and sympathy with the beauty of reason.)

The Rose Tree Estate did try to provide beauty and fair works, but the feeling, deep within a person, that their value was not enough to keep their parents alongside them, at least until they were mature enough to go it alone, was a cut so deep. If your mother does not want you; that is a much, much, much bigger scar than the removal of the appendix.

It was not only the children and young people, the 'inmates' of this strange microcosm, that had difficulties -- far from it. Many of the staff had their own issues with the things that had happened to them in their lives. Indeed, there were, amongst the staff, people who had been in care themselves. Those who had were generally empathetic, although some took the view that life is tough, and only the tough survive, so we better help the helpless and make them strong. 'How do you become strong?' they would question. 'By having to fight.' was their answer. These people could make anyone's life a living hell.

There were individuals, among the staff, whose self-image was so low that they were a grave danger to any of the children in the care of Rose Tree. Sadly, in the cut and thrust of making everything work to a budget, and keeping the show on the road, observation of disreputable behaviour was easily missed, and at times, brushed under the carpet for fear of rocking the boat and sending it off course. There were many alliances, many secrets, which kept a ghastly engine of malice chuntering on through the weeks, years, and generations. Some people avoided this nastiness, others were destroyed by it. To balance this dark and sinister underbelly, were those house-parents who were of good self-esteem, who were working to try and make the lives of their charges better, and with every effort they made, they were able to help many through their difficulties and prepare them for the big-wide-world to live reasonable and decent lives.

Chapter 10

Content With Destiny Isoken

Narrator

Nigerian troops entered Biafra on the sixth July nineteen-sixty-seven. Circumstance had it that Isoken, and her family, who were from Benin, found themselves amid the Nigerian-Biafran War. Isoken witnessed many acts of brutality, barbarity and death. She saw starving, emaciated bodies, salt starved Kwashiorkor people, children with swollen legs and empty swollen tummies, and oh how hungry she was. People ate lizards, people ate rats, she learned that when you have to, you can do many things that maybe you otherwise would not want to. She learned to eat tasteless, salt-free, food. Sometimes they were lucky, they would find some, terrible tasting, Gabon beans, corn, maybe peas and some fat, from a soldier's rations. When they were even luckier, they would spot a kernel beneath a palm tree. They moved from village-to-village Obimo, Nkpologu, on and on. There was no school but Isoken learned how to shoot a gun, and she had shot and killed a soldier. Her father's second wife died of a fever. One-by-one her eleven siblings succumbed and were left where they died as there was no way to leave them in dignity. She was so young and knew fear so well.

Her fortune was that her father had had success in life and was not so poor as many of the people Isoken had seen on this terrible journey. However, money has no value when there was nothing to exchange it for, and there was nothing -- absolutely nothing -- anywhere on the journey the family had taken. Her father had used his connections to secure passage for the family out of Nigeria as stowaway passengers on an oil tanker. Isoken's father became a victim of the conflict, so it was only her mother, and this, pre-pubescent teenager, who embarked secretly in the dark. The tanker had lumbered across the Gulf of Guinea, out into the Atlantic, hugging the coast of West Africa, passing between it and Gran Canaria, via Morocco and Portugal, skirting the Bay of Biscay and on to England, it seemed to Isoken that they had been aboard the oil tanker forever. They had not been uncomfortable on the journey except for the seasickness. The person who had smuggled them on board had kept them supplied with food and drink. They were able to wash; they had even been given some clothes to wear. Isoken did not know how much her father had paid the smugglers. She realised that there were a good number of people involved in the deception, and each must have been given a substantial reward to ensure their complete cooperation. Her mother had told her that when the boat had reached England and they were safely ashore, the smugglers would be able to collect a final payment for their services. She told Isoken to remember exactly what the instructions were, in case anything she happen to her. Under no circumstances should Isoken tell them where to get their money. Only when she was safely out of the docks and in England she should then take one of the smugglers to get the last payment. As she memorised all that her mother said, she did not know that her mother would die on the ship before they arrived in England. It started like a cold but in a few days Isoken's mother was fighting a raging fever. When Isoken woke in the morning she found that her mother was no longer breathing. Later one of the men took Isoken away from the cabin. She was able to watch the endless sea for a while, and breathe in the negative ions on the breeze, her body felt refreshed, but her heart was heavy for the loss of her mother, and the fear of the unknown. She was strong, and had seen such a catalogue of horror, but even so this was a very tough day. When they returned, her mother's body was no longer there, Isoken never saw her mother again, she had never been so alone. The smugglers were gentle people, they were not people traffickers, they were some people involved in her father's business activities, this was a bit of extra, illicit, cash with a humanitarian edge. Isoken did exactly as her mother had said. One of the men went with her, he got the final payment from a grumpy, elderly, scruffy man, after Isoken had given him a password, and had answered two questions. Isoken was surprised that it was so easy. The Smuggler left her around the corner from a police station. He said;

"I think you are a very brave young woman, the people here cannot know it was us who bought you here, you do understand?"

Isoken replied. "Yes of course."

She wiped a tear from her eye. "Thank you."

He said. "I am sorry I have to leave you, but I would be in serious trouble if I do any more. You will be alright here, the police are mostly good here, there is no war, and there is plenty of food and you can drink the water straight from a tap! Many houses have bathrooms with toilets inside the house! Go into the police station and say you need asylum."

Isoken had no idea how to tell the people in Sycamore House, on The Rose Tree Estate, all of that. There was so much that she could not share. She screwed the lid on tight. Some of the other kids in the house, where she had been put, thought that she was the wrong colour and because she was not communicating with them; they attacked her in any way they could. Until one day she exploded and Adam Martin got the beating of his life. He had been brought up the hard-way; his father knocked more than seven bells out of him before he was ten. Now, as a lanky, just, teenager, he thought he was King of this Jungle. As Isoken's fist smashed into his teeth he realised that he had just met Jane, and she fought like a lioness, she had him pinned to the floor, whilst all the other kids stood with their mouths open, drooling for more violence. She was screaming at Adam in French, none of them knew what she was saying, but Adam's nose had blood trickling from it and he had lost by a hefty margin. Damien Marshall began to laugh he shouted.

"Isoken's a witch she's putting a spell on Adam."

Damien was trying to be clever, he had a notion that Witch Doctors were something to be feared. He had heard that somewhere and he had an idea that such people came from Africa. So the chant sprang up.

"Isoken's a witch, Isoken's a witch….." It got louder and louder. Adam was crushed by this event. His life was not much, it never had been, but here in this house he had been *'Tarzan the King'* for a while, he had been the bully of the common room, what was his status now? He was lost. Isoken released him. The chanting went quiet, and both the gladiators left the battlefield to weep under the covers on their beds. Isoken heard her mother's voice through the pillow.

"It will seem better in the morning." All the way through that dreadful war, her mother would say that as they tried to sleep. Every morning they woke and it always seemed the same. The words had kept them going. "Words are powerful things." Isoken could hear her mother clearly through the pillow. Words can change the world.

Adam had not cried for years, why would he? His father would slap him if he cried, and his mother never stopped his brutal father, for she was as scared as Adam. Adam cried himself to sleep.

Chapter 11
Session Five: An Away-Day with the Doctor
Kristopher

It was time for my fifth session with Doctor Samuels. I had started to think about when I was going to tell him.

"There was a girl called Rose...."

Then I remembered that it was pilgrimage time and we were supposed to go together to see The Rose Tree Estate. Rose was foremost in my thoughts.

"When Rose came to stay -- my dad told me this many years later -- she did not want to stay. She was very nervous. Her father had died in the very last part of the Second World War, he never knew that Rose was to be born. Rose was the youngest of thirteen siblings, she was born into a flattened East End of London and grow up playing in the ruins. Finally, her mother could cope no longer and several of the children were taken in to the care of the various institutions.

The first home that Rose went to was full of girls around eleven and twelve years-old. Things were homely and the house-parents were kind. The girls, for the main part, got on together really well. School took up a lot of the day, and then there was bathing, dressing, eating and sometimes school homework. The care home had a large garden with lawns, apple trees and flowerbeds, roses and quince. Rose actually loved the first months there. Then a new member of staff arrived. He bought with him some of the discipline of his time in the army during the war. He believed in regimenting the girls and he would bark orders at them. He would ensure they had tidy rooms, made beds, and that they had cleaned until there was not a speck of dust anywhere. These things, in themselves were not to the detriment of the young people, indeed many learned a lot and they all learned something of discipline. However, there was more to his motivation that having to earn a living. Yvonne was the first to say something. She said it to Heather at breakfast when Mr. Smith was not on duty. When she knew that the housemother would hear her. Yvonne said;

"Have you noticed how Mr. Smith always hangs around the bathrooms at bath time?"

Heather said. "Yes and he walked in on me and Rose."

Rose said. "That's not all."

At this point the housemother said: "Rose I wonder if you could help me a moment."

They left the room for a short time. Nothing more was said. They did not see Mr. Smith again. It was shortly after this that Rose was sent to join us at Nut Tree House. The place where my dad and mum were in charge.

My dad told me that Rose did not want to stay. She had been disturbed by the actions of Mr. Smith and she missed the girls she had befriended at the other place. She had the idea that she was being punished for what

Mr. Smith had done -- but she had done nothing wrong.

Rose told me that my dad had said to her;

"Look the doors are not locked, I cannot keep you here, but if you want to stay, my wife, the staff and I will look after you."

It was around that moment that I arrived on the scene. I had heard the end of this conversation and walking into the room I said;

"I will play with you!"

Rose laughed, and I said. "I like it here. My name is Kristopher. What is your name?"

"I am Rose. I like your name." She said.

"I said: "Well I think this is your home Rose, this Nut Tree House on The ROSE Tree Estate. I am hungry Daddy."

So we all went to the kitchen.

I told all that to the kindly doctor as he drove to The Rose Tree Estate.

The streets were suddenly filled with familiarity, and time in its snake-like coils bought my nearly retired self in direct contact with the little boy of three and four years old, who had, safely, wandered about these places with little care, with parents who had enveloped my life in the love and care. Care that had not smothered, care that had enabled me to reach a robust adulthood. I was sure that as much as I did not notice my parents, in my every day wanderings, sixty years ago, they were keeping their eyes on me, if they were not, how would my dad have taken me up in his arms as I reached the top of the hill opposite the library on the day I had ridden my tricycle on that adventure? Now I could see him following behind, ducking behind the post box, sneaking quickly into the shop doorway, giving me the feeling that I was free, yet there he was -- watching over me, keeping me safe. What luck was I born into, so opposite was my fortune from so many of the unfortunate lost boys and girls who inhabited the houses of The Rose Tree Estate. In later years I came to know that any who fell into the care of my mum and my dad immediately found safety. For they were both secure with in themselves and they were solid and secure as a couple.

My dad's and mum's security came from their firm belief in The Lord Jesus Christ and his Father, whom they called their God. They did not shout and scream about their beliefs, and indeed, I was unaware of them all through my childhood. Except for the visits to Sunday School, and to church, but to me that seemed to be what people did, it was normal. Of course back then it was very normal, things have changes over the six decades of my life, indeed, my own self-confidence is not wrapped up in a belief in any supranatural force, in the same way as was theirs. Indeed the day I moved out of my dad's house, and into my own, he said to me.

"I have shown you my life, you know exactly what I think about most things. However, this is your life and what you do with it is totally up to you." I have only ever been to church when it was an occasion that one had to, weddings and funerals.

You think about that. What self-confidence, what deep self-belief. I know I had been one of the luckiest persons to have ever been born when I consider what was said to me on that day.

Just at that moment the doctor's car pulled up at the traffic lights. I said.

"That is the Library, it is unchanged. Over on that corner is where I rode my tricycle on that day. Over on that corner was the bubble gum machine my aunty would not let me use. She said she had seen a nasty boy lift the door from which the bubble gumball would come, and the boy had spat into it. I never used one of those machines again in my life."

The lights were still red and I said, "Izzy wizzy, let's get busy on the magic green light". The words flowed as they had done when my dad taught me them so many years before. As the word 'lights' left my tongue, the traffic lights did change to green. We drove on down the hill passing some houses on the left whilst there were still some shops that were recognisable from nineteen fifty-eight. The Garage was now a hand car washing place and there were two take away kebab shops, I do not think there were kebab shops back in the day. There was a Post Office, which I do not remember being there. The barber was now Turkish, or so it could be read on the sign, my favourite 'Grubber' sweetie shop was now a funeral business, but the one across the street was still there, it was now a newspaper shop, and the signage above blurted out in purple and yellow; 'Premier Store'. The doctor and I stepped up to the door, I said;

"You know I am really tempted to ask if they have those tubes with the lovely tasting goo in them, but I know they would think me off my head if I were to do so."

It was not the same shop at all, of course the people who ran it in nineteen fifty-eight were most probably away to heaven, or wherever their faith told them they would go.

Next came the big test. I had asked the doctor if we could cross the road at the zebra crossing and walk along to the traffic lights by the newspaper shop. We would then be exactly opposite the gates and the gate-lodge, where I had been shown how to draw a straight line with a round black ruler that was probably a roller from an old type writer.

"Do you remember any of your classics, Doctor Samuels?"

"Sorry I am not sure of what you are asking." Puzzled the doctor.

"Socrates, Plato and that kind of stuff?" I mused.

"No, I cannot say I have any speed at all in that direction." The doctor looked a little embarrassed.

"One of Socrates' phrases, so they say, was; 'The only thing I know is that I know nothing'. Quite some thought that. I suppose that we all only know the little bit we know, from our point of view, and that little bit is hardly a grain of sand on the beach of all that has gone on in the universe over the past thirteen and a half billion years. Plato left behind many sayings and phrases. One of his ideas was that youth should be surrounded by fair works, sounds and beauty. I wonder if that is where they got the idea for making The Rose Tree Estate so beautiful. I tell you Doctor Samuels, when I lived there it was beautiful. Trees and shrubs, green lawns, and white picket fences. Plato said that knowledge, that is facts, is different from belief, or maybe I should say opinion. It is possible for a fact to be the same as the opinion people have about it.... You look puzzled again doctor, let me give you an example. The red traffic light back there by the library, in your opinion was the red light red or green?"

"Red, of course."

"Yes, and that can be proven, because we can compare that red with a light spectrum and calculate its frequency. So the opinion, and the belief are the same as the fact, the knowledge, in this case. Plato said that knowledge, facts, have to account for themselves, they have to have proofs. So we thank Isaac Newton for introducing science to the rainbow and to all the other scientists who have given values to all the frequencies in the spectrum so we now have the benefit of knowing that the colour red has a frequency of four-hundred to four-hundred and eighty terahertz, it can be proven. How, my dear doctor, can we say that beauty is fact, or is it always opinion? How could beauty prove itself? Plato said that even things, that most people might have the opinion are fact, may not be fact at all! Could the lines I drew, in that building, over there, when I was three years old, actually have really been straight? Are plates really round? Can there be a perfect circle? Or do we accept things are near enough straight or round? The lines we draw have also breadth, the only truly straight line, maybe, the one you and I can see in our mind's eye from point to point. Maybe our eyes only witness approximations of what are really facts."

"Wow." Said the doctor, "What brought all that on?"

"Well I looked across the road just then, and with all my memories -- the facts, as I like to see them -- I remembered that as a happy place, but suppose another person came along with a different idea in their head, they might hear themselves saying. 'Abandon Hope All Ye Who Enter Here.' Or *'Arbeit Macht Frie'*, 'Work Makes Free'."

This vision was one of the strongest I had of The Rose Tree Estate, for me it was a wonderful place full of excitement and adventure. Looking across the street now, with the doctor beside me, I wondered how it had seemed to the children who had been forced to live there during all the years that it was open. It had started as a private charitable institution to care to destitute children. It then fell into the care of the London County Council, until that was done away with.

In nineteen sixty-five, and the The Greater London Council took over until nineteen eighty-three when Mrs. Thatcher closed that, because she loathed Ken Livingstone and his progressive Labour Party regime.

We crossed the road, peered through the window of the lodge, there were net curtains.

"Someone must live in there now." I said. "That was the house in which I had my first memories. Nut Tree House. I found the photograph I mentioned the other week." I put my hand into the inside pocket of my jacket and pulled out an envelope. I took the photograph from it and showed it to the doctor. "I was sitting on the grass there, look you can see the Keepers Lodge with the Bedford van parked before it. Over there," I pointed, "Was a white picket fence around a cottage, I think it was where one of the staff lived."

When we came to the back of the house, the old toilet block was still standing. "Well they had installed toilets in the house by the time I remember them so they were not used then. They are all locked." I said as I tried the door handles.

We walked all over the estate, past the other houses and the swimming pool and the laundry had been. The Rose Tree Estate closed its doors in nineteen eighty-three and since then some of the houses, the pool and laundry had gone. Some of the big houses had been turned in to elegant apartments for the well heeled. One compete house was now a big house for a very wealthy family. There were also some smart townhouses, which had been built, recently. Even with all that change the place was still recognisable. My brain was flushed with many more memories than I had before.

"That is where the greenhouses were. They were very large. Brick walls at the bottom then window lights in a white wooden frames above." I pointed again.

The doctor said; "Good, good. I think it is time to go back to the car now."

Chapter 12
Gordon Gabon
Narrator

Of course they all called him GG, and there were endless jokes about horses, betting, hay and stables. The children in Hazel House, on The Rose Tree Estate in nineteen fifty-eight, used to tell a joke, they all thought it rude, and very naughty. Not so much a joke, maybe, more of a rhyme, 'I82CAGGP' is what they chanted. It was all light-hearted and taken in good spirit.

As much as many who arrived on The Rose Tree Estate, were lost and bewildered, many more arrived with relief that their suffering had been stemmed, that they now had a water-tight roof overhead, three meals a day, clean clothes and adults around them that provided security and assurance. Humans need to be warm and dry, they need a couple of thousand calories a day, and they need to feel safe. Safety brings freedom, provided there is not some regressive Government intent on protecting its limited ideology.

The above is not to suggest that new arrivals did not have to get used to their new habitat, nor that there were not difficulties in some getting beyond the trauma of the path that had led them to Rose Tree.

The Rose Tree Estate was full of worthy, kindly, good, people who worked tirelessly for the health and well-being of their charges. People who would always do more than was required by their contract of employment. Indeed, the vast majority, maybe ninety-eight to ninety-nine per cent of the staff, were of the mind that they wanted the world to be a better place. For gardeners to cooks, maintenance people to laundry workers, accountants to secretaries, matrons to wardens; that was why they were working there. That and the need to earn their living of course. Many had survived the Second World War, many had lost loved ones, friends, and colleagues, and some had barely escaped their own deaths. The last thing on Earth any of these people would seek to do would be to harm another person, least of all a child who was in their care, a child to whom they were in *loco parentis*. Most of these fine people were the best of humanity. They were people who would laugh, dry the tears answer the questions. They would ensure that baths were taken and homework was done. They were people who would break up fights and help settle disputes, they would read bedtime stories and watch over their little ones at night. You see there is a thing about history, so often historians teach of battles, hardship and torture, famines and death. It is easy to think 'well if it were all so bad why did people keep going on and making more babies? If it were all so terrible why were there no mass suicides?' Of course the answer is; for all the pain there was also much joy, and people always hope for joy. Indeed, without the optimism that things will be better tomorrow, how would anyone carry on? It is so easy to look at something and find the one percent that does not work, whilst ignoring the ninety-nine percent which functions perfectly.

George Gabon was the representation of the ninety-nine percent that worked perfectly. He was a lovely man. In nineteen fifty-eight George was forty-three years old. On the eighth of November, nineteen fifty-eight the children, aged eight to twelve years old, had just sung *Happy Birthday* to George, and George had blown out the candles on the cake which Cook had baked for the celebration. There was a cheer and someone started;

'For he's a jolly good fellow, for he's a jolly good fellow,
for he's a jolly good fellow and so say all of us.'

There was clapping and laughing, and then someone put on a record it was Cliff Richard & The Drifters, *Move It*. Everyone started jumping and dancing around. George could hardly believe it, for him this was a moment to savour. For his life had not always been as good as this. No indeed. His father had left his mother before she knew she was pregnant. His mother had been disowned by her family; and oh how she had to struggle. She did struggle -- and she survived. She told people that her husband had died. She worked, but it was not easy. George was loved and cared for in the best way his mother knew. In nineteen fifteen the effects of the First World War were all too apparent upon the population of England. George was twenty-four when the Second World War started. He joined the Royal Navy. In a strange turn of fate, he found himself in a part of the conflict involving the country which shared his name; The Gabon, in Africa. Charles De Gaulle had set about operations to attack The Vichy-Government held territories in French Equatorial Africa. The British Navy was providing support. George was on board the *HMS Devonshire* and he was a mechanic who helped keep the *Supermarine Walrus* biplane in operation. So on his birthday, eighteen years before, this nineteen fifty-eight birthday celebration, George had been there when the plane was launched and bombed a Vichy submarine the *Poncelet*. The Walrus was an amazing craft. It was launched by catapult from the deck of the *Devonshire*. Working so closely with the aircraft gave George a feeling of pride. Every time the craft was flicked into the air he knew he was one of the few who could enable the bird to fly. George was in Scapa Flow in nine forty-four and in nineteen forty-five the *Devonshire* was in The Norwegian Sea. So George did get to see a lot of the world, from the Indian Ocean to the South Atlantic, and all the way to Australia. George stayed as a member of the crew until The *Devonshire* was converted into a training ship in nineteen forty-seven.

The winter of nineteen forty-seven was a huge shock for George's system, back from the tropics to the heaviest snowfall that had been recorded in Britain.

Having survived the war, George almost did not survive a car crash on an isolated snow and ice-bound road in Bedfordshire. The luck George had on the day was that a farmer, with a tractor, witnessed the accident and was able to come to the aid of the victims. Fortunately, George made it out alive, to a hospital, but both his legs had to be amputated.

It took a lot of time to recover, but eventually George mastered his artificial legs and thought of himself as a kind of *Douglas Bader*. He trained to be a teacher. Later he saw an advertisement for a house-parent post on The Rose Tree Estate. There he found a place that he felt needed him as much as he needed it. He worked there until his retirement in nineteen eighty. No one had a bad word to say about George, and George never said a bad word about anyone. He was dedicated to his work and he cared for every detail. He made sure that every child in care in Hazel House was looked after. That meant that most of the time he was smiling and happy, but occasionally he could be assertive if it was necessary to maintain, or restore order, or to ensure that a new arrival felt secure. George was reliable he always meant what he said and said what he meant. George, and all those he cared for, knew that sometimes the answer would be 'no'. If George said no, he meant no. Security is born within proper boundaries, and so the children felt that they were loved.

In nineteen fifty-six, Anthony came to live in Hazel House. Anthony had contracted Polio, he was an orphan. He wore spectacles with thick glass which gave his eyes a peculiar un-gainly squint. He looked shabby and underfed when he arrived. His right leg was held stiff by a leather and metal leg brace. Another boy, Ted, who had arrived only the day before, started to pick on Anthony as soon as he had hobbled through the door. The tension between the two-ten-year olds rose and rose throughout the day when finally Anthony snapped and chased Ted into a corner. Anthony then kicked Ted and kicked him hard. It took three of the house-parents to break up the fight. At teatime, the children sat around their tables and George asked Anthony and Ted to come to the front. The boys stood, one to George's right and the other to his left. Then George said;

"These two boys are new to Hazel House, *pay attention Simon, and stop fidgeting Jane*.... what I have to say is important. Ted you have spent most of the day trying to wind Anthony up, and I would like to know why?"

Ted shuffled his feet uncomfortably.

"Come on speak up now." Said George.

Ted said in defiant tone: "Well look at him, gawky-eyed git with a metal leg."

George replied: "Well I see you have a problem with Anthony's glasses. Without them Anthony could not see, he has had problems with his eyes since he was born. You Ted, you are very lucky for you can see clearly with no need for glasses. Just suppose an accident were to befall you and your eyes were damaged and you then needed to wear glasses"

Ted looked straight ahead and said nothing. George continued, "Nobody in this room knows this. In March nineteen forty-seven I was in a car accident. That car accident almost killed me. I was very lucky because a farmer came and managed to rescue me from the wreck and he got me to a hospital. I remained there for a long time because they had to cut off both my legs."

At this Polly, a ten-year-old girl, let out a yelp and every one turned to look at her.

"So how can you stand there GG?" Called out Gary.

Beverly said: "How can you walk?"

George said: "My legs are made of metal."

Sally-Anne said, "I don't believe you."

"Well come over here Sally-Anne." Said George.

Sally Anne stood up from the table and walked across the room.

George said: "Tap on my right shin with your hand, like you are knocking on a door."

Sally-Anne knelt down, she hesitated.

George said: "Not too hard I do not want you to hurt me."

There was silence and then Shirley laughed. She said: "If your leg is metal it cannot hurt you if Sally-Anne knocks on it."

George said: "You are right Shirley, Sally-Anne should not knock too hard otherwise she might hurt her hand. Go on Sally-Anne everyone is hungry."

Sally-Anne did as she was told and then let out a yelp. "GG your leg is metal!"

George said: "I have never, and I will never, tell you a lie. Knock on the other one. Now I have been walking on these metal legs for nine years. Better stand up now Sally-Anne. These metal legs of mine start on the soles of my metal feet and go right up to beyond my knees. None of you knew, none of the house-parents knew of my metal legs until now, you just thought that I walk funny. Ted, I know a lot about you, because I have read all the papers about you. We all have problems; Anthony has two big problems that are visible to everyone. There is no need to point out other people's problems, hoping that they will not see your problems. We all have problems. You, Ted, attack before you get attacked, I understand that, and I understand why you are defensive. What I can assure you of is this, whilst you are here, in Hazel House, with me, you do not need to be defensive, for as I am now defending Anthony, I will equally defend you. Now I know that might sound strange to you Ted, but things are different here, you are safe here with the other house-parents and with me. So calm down and relax. Cook has prepared tea. Go and sit up at your places Anthony and Ted. Now hands together, eyes closed, don't forget to blow your nose."

This joke was repeated at every mealtime, and it always raised a smile.

Then George said: "Sally-Anne well you please say the Grace?"

"For what we are about to receive may the Lord make us truly thankful."

Chapter 13
Session Six: Security
Kristopher

"I did not know why she did not want to stay. It puzzled me, why would anybody not want to stay there?"

"You are speaking of Rose, Kristopher." Interrupted Doctor Samuels.

"Yes." I said. "I think my dad and mum made her feel secure. I think that is what they did for all those in their care. They did the same for me, I was allowed to be myself, even at that age, because they were secure in themselves, and that transferred to me. No one filled my head with danger, consequently there was little danger. They figured that I would know that the fire was hot because I could feel it, no need keep on about it then.

On Bonfire night there was a big fire, someone showed me how to write my name in the air with a sparkler. My dad lit Catherine wheels and there were loud bangs.

There was snow and sun, the girls made an ice-slide. The scene was like the picture on the cover of a knitting pattern that my Granny used when making a jumper or scarf. Am I repeating myself?

One snowy day there was a squirrel on the windowsill of the bedroom, which I shared with my baby brother. He slept in a cot, I had a bed. I had a wooden toy, it was constructed in an H shape. The horizontal plank had holes in it, and in the holes were wooden pegs, each was coloured, red, blue, green, yellow. There was a wooden hammer and it was used to hammer the pegs through the holes, and then turn it over and hammer them through again.

I was ill and had to take a nasty tasting tablet. My mum pushed it into a chocolate sweet and I ate it.

The house was heated by coal fires in grates in each room. My dad always built fires in the same way; sticks of kindling wood arranged as a square tower. Newspaper rolled into a tube and then tied in a knot under the wood. The paper would be ignited by a match. The coal added, once the kindling was alight, it was tossed into the flames.

My dad kept several large scrapbooks, maybe the size of a broadsheet newspaper, but thicker. They were full of a thick grey paper called sugar-paper. I, too, was encouraged to cut out pictures and stick them into my own scrapbook. Here is one anomaly of these young years; although I was free to roam unsupervised, although I was allowed to walk up to my nursery school alone alongside a busy main road, although there were fireplaces with no guards -- the issue of the scrapbook bought out some reptilian fears for my safety from within my mum. My mum gave me some scissors to cut out things for the scrapbook. They were made from some sort of Bakelite, a type of hard plastic, and completely useless. I had noticed that my Granddad had lost the tip of his middle finger, he said the accident happened when he was gardening with a pair of shears. I thought well he could not of done it himself, so who was using the shears? I never found out, but could it have been my own mum? Now, wracked with guilt, worried about her son's fingers? Anyway it was not to long before real pair of scissors was made available. At the time of writing this, sixty years later, I have, still, the fortune of eight fingers and two thumbs. That is amazing really.

If any one is reading this, and they were born into the nineteen nineties, or there about, in the United Kingdom, you may be horrified by some of the things you have already read. Think again, childhood is a luxury that many generations before us could not enjoy. Children were sent up chimneys and down into coalmines, they were sold into slavery. Charles Kingsley's book *The Water Babies* was started in eighteen sixty-two. My great-grandparents were alive then. As I said before, I was fortunate to know them, and I knew them well. I will tell of visits to stay with my granny shortly, but this fits in here. From a very tender age, when staying at her house, one job I was given to do was to chop the wood for the kindling. For this work I would be given an axe, similar to a machete, and I could easily spend a number of hours hacking and smashing away in the back garden. It was normal!

You may think I am making all of this up, but really, I can remember all these things as if they happened yesterday."

Doctor Samuels interrupted me: "Kristopher, I can assure you that I do respect, and believe, all that you have been telling me. After our visit to The Rose Tree Estate I can see the whole story unfolding. I do hope that soon you will find the confidence in me, that you need, to divulge that deep, and troublesome knot which is still deep within your psyche. Kristopher, this is our sixth session and you are doing so well. You do have a remarkable recall, better than any I have before dealt with before. Please continue."

The doctor was silent for a few moments and so was I. I was searching, scanning those corridors where the cages were where I had kept all those darkness's of the past. It may have been a full two minutes before I was able to continue. When I opened my mouth it was not the things in the cages that escaped, but more of the banal, the everyday things, the things that cluttered and blocked in the evil.

"Other things that come to mind are visions of the huge kitchen and the high table in the middle of it, the stools around it, all to high for me to deal with. I remember Margaret Fates, who worked with my dad and mum, caring for the girls; I remember her smile and her tiny, neat, handwriting. The kitchen was in constant use for normal meal preparations and sometimes there would be jam or toffee making. Maybe it was of my mum's experiences of rationing during the Second World War, that she always made sure that there were stocks of food, and that meals were plentiful.

You know scientists studied the diet of maladjusted children in American prisons. They found that many of the unruly ate a poor diet. The scientists provided a multi-vitamin pill and the behaviour of these youngsters improved. Maybe my dad and mum already worked that out all those years before.

Another memory of the kitchen was the traps for wasps. Insects were much more plentiful in the nineteen fifties. At the end of the summer there would be hundreds of wasps to deal with, not to eradicate them, just to keep then away from the human food and minimise the possibility of stings. So empty jam jars were part-filled with a little sugary water, the lid was put on and a hole was made in the lid, about big enough for the wasps to crawl in but difficult for them to get out. A lot were caught. In those days, if we drove out to the countryside in the car, at night, thousands of moths could be seen flying into the headlights of the car. Not now. Indeed even in the ninety eighties and nineties driving the car through the summer would cause millions of insects to adhere to the front of any car and be very difficult to clean off.

I went Sunday school. They gave me a book at Christmas, with a label in the front, on which was written my name and something about a good attendance record, my dad told me. The label was not hard fixed and I pealed it off to find another label beneath, I could not read it and my dad was confused for there was a different name on the label beneath! Then there was church - I remember being there at weddings. My parents seemed to try and marry off as many of the girls that were in their care as soon they could. My granny was there, and I remember my aunt Susan there on one occasion, they had fur coats, and my cousin Sharon, and I, would find ourselves wrapped in the coats and around their legs if we stood close to either of them. Just our faces peering out into the cold of the winter.

There was also my nursery school. It was a short walk away. Leaving out of the main gate, I would turn right up the slope for a hundred yards, turn right and into the village hall. I often made this journey unsupervised, and returned home alone too. We would sing and paint, *Insy-Winsy-Spider.* Sometimes we would go into the Nissen-Hut, located behind the hall, for games, usually when it was raining. The noise on the corrugated iron enclosure was quite something. (Nissen-Huts were a semi-circle of corrugated iron with door and windows to the front, sometimes the rear, and sometimes with a window in the side. They were an easily erected building invented by Peter Nissen during the First World War.) We played 'In and Out the Dusty Blue Bells', 'Farmer's in His Den', 'Poor Jenny is a

Weeping', 'Here we go round the Mulberry Bush'. 'Stuck in the Mud' etc. etc. I remember going to a birthday party for one of the other children and I can remember the room in which the party was, we played, 'Pin the Tail on the Donkey' and 'Pass the Parcel', and I also remember something of the tea.

One girl, from the nursery was very pretty and it was arranged that she would come for tea with me at Nut Tree House. I remember that day was extraordinarily long, waiting, and waiting, from the time I woke up until, finally, she arrived in the late afternoon. We played with some long cardboard tubes that had once had carpets rolled around them, the carpet having been, used leaving the cardboard tubes. Inside these tubes were discs of wood designed to keep the tube ridged. The girl and I spent most of our time together extracting these discs from several of the tubes.

There was another girl in my life at that time, I remember her name; Gillian, she was the daughter of someone my parents knew, she had a younger brother too. I remember us playing with my toys on the front lawn. This must have been after my dad's parents had been to stay. They came all the way from Uganda. My Grandfather drove the trains there. He bought me a clockwork train set. It was wide-gauge made from tin. Gillian and I played with this train set. Many children had, toys made of tin in those days, 'Made in Hong Kong' stamped on many of them. There were toy cars, and spinning tops which hummed if you managed to get them spinning fast enough.

Chapter 14
Malcolm
Narrator

Malcolm had nothing to do with The Rose Tree Estate, but his wife was a house-parent in one of the houses there. Her name was Ivy. She was very competent, 'a safe pair of hands', a person who was experienced and good at her job. She had worked in Aspen House, on The Rose Tree Estate for seven years. Aspen House took in particularly boisterous individuals. Young people who might have been candidates for Borstal but they had been given the opportunity to take advantage of the experience of Ivy and her co-workers. The work was far from easy. Young people in their teens, hormones raging, as they transition to adulthood. All from very difficult backgrounds, all suffering a lack of love and stability. Many had suffered abuse of one kind or another. It was easy for such youngsters to mistake love for sex, and thus evil people found it easy to take advantage. Ivy was pleased with the work she did but for all the time and attention, she felt, many really did not benefit a great deal. Much of the time Ivy and her colleagues were in crisis management mode, for there was always some individual who had got in to some terrible situation and needed to be helped out.

Malcolm worked at another establishment, a Secure Unit. One step away from being a young offenders prison. Malcolm often said to Ivy that he did not understand why Aspen house existed, as many of it's patrons would later end up as his guests. "Sooner or later." He would often say.

Malcolm should never have been given his job. He was too inadequate within himself. The lack of self-assuredness meant he knew everything about everything and would offer, free, advice on any subject you would care to name. He grew a beard because he thought it made him look older and more experienced. In reality, the boys in the Secure Unit used to laugh at his baby features and make fun of him, by pretending to stroke non-existent beards upon their own faces. Malcolm was uncomfortable in himself and let everyone about him know it. That was a big problem for the young men who fell into his care, for such young men require a role model, a figure to look up to, someone who does not need to throw threats around a room. The young men in Malcolm's care needed to know that the person caring for them could whip the hide of any of them, or even all of them at the same time, but that he never would, because they, and he, knew he did not have to. Deep-seated self-confidence that commands the room, and makes everyone know things are all right, no one needs to be in fear. So much of what humans do is through fear. The two great motivators are greed and fear. Fear, though is what most people cling onto because they do not want to be hurt again. They keep a great catalogue of things that have done them harm in their past, and they use most of their energy holding their shields up so no one can get in and hurt them again. Malcolm barked out his orders trying to be the hard man that he was not. When really what these boys needed was the love of a proper father, who would praise the good, and admonish the bad, and who would smile and have fun in-between times.

So conflicts often erupted. Malcolm, and his colleagues would wade into the affray, throwing their weight around, using the techniques they had been taught to constrain, and remove, a troublemaker and place them into solitary confinement until things had cooled down. Often these solitary times just allowed a temper to brew and become stronger and more contagious. Malcolm and his colleagues, more often that not, did far more damage than they did good.

Ivy was not interested in working in a Secure Unit she just wanted to keep as many young people away from Malcolm, and his colleagues, as she could. She thought that people always have more good in them than bad, and that the bad was often a manifestation of the fear people felt.

What Ivy saw in Malcolm, as a husband, was a mystery to most, they seemed incompatible. She being *petit* and easy to look at, he tall, with a demeanour which made many wish to turn away. That may have been the very thing which drew them together, for they were quite opposite to one another. They were married and Ivy put up with Malcolm for five years, but after that she could put up with it no more, and they went their separate ways.

Chapter 15
Rose
Narrator

When Rose came to live at The Rose Tree Estate, she had already experienced, at another care home, the evil of a man who wished to gain sexual gratification from young girls, who were in his care, and whom he should have protected. The man lost his job when Rose and her pal, Heather, reported that Mr. Smith had tried to look at them whilst they were naked in the bathroom. Losing his job was the only consequence, that, and a reference, which was far from glowing, but did not mention that which was unmentionable.

Rose was far from innocent at the age of fourteen, when Kristopher's parents started caring for her. Born in nineteen forty-four, as the Second World War was in its final year, it was in the wreckage of East London that she had her first memories. Her father never knew her; he was killed in the very last part of the war, a British Soldier who was, sadly the victim of a bomb which was dropped on Germany, by the Royal Air Force. So, Rose and her twelve siblings knew much hardship, her mother did what she could, all of the children did what they could. She had learned from her eldest sister, Edith, that money could be obtained by letting a boy, or even a man, have a 'kiss and a fumble'. Edith showed Rose what to do and told her what *not* to do. The danger was on a sliding scale of how hungry Edith, Rose and their family happened to be.

Edith told Rose: "Always get the money first. Never let one of them put it in you, they don't need to, if you rub them enough it happens in your hand. You just have to let them know you'll never do anything with them again if they try anything. Just in case keep this nail in your left hand and stab it in their leg if they try anything. Only use this alley for business, you can easily run down here and one of us will be waiting to help if needed."

Society often considers children to be vulnerable, that is often because people keep children in ignorance. Rose was possibly the least vulnerable of souls as Edith provided full, and intimate details of every aspect of the way she was able to make a living. Rose listened, watched, and learned. This group of youngsters worked as a pack and they were actually as safe as it was possible to be in such circumstances. Nonetheless, when their mother got sick, and the pressure was too much, some of her children moved into the care of the welfare state.

Rose stayed at Nut Tree House, on The Rose Tree Estate, for around three or four years. In that time she learned to read and write, then she got a job working at *Barretts*, a big department store in the town. At the age of seventeen, she met a young man of nineteen. They fell in love and got married. Kristopher's mum made the wedding cake; Kristopher's dad walked the bride up the aisle of the church. He also put white ribbons on his old car, and someone tied tin cans on strings to the back bumper and wrote a sign, on cardboard, Just Married and tied it to the back of the car. Rose was the first Nut Tree girl to get married. At the time it seemed like a reasonable strategy, to get these young women wed before they were obliged to leave the care of the council. For some of the girls it was a good thing, at least two of them married and lived happily ever after. They had children and fine lives.

Rose's marriage was fine for a while, five years actually. She was twenty-two and Bruce was twenty-four. They were living in a council flat, in a nineteen sixty-six, in a tower block. The World Cup was won and Bobby Moore, the English football Captain, held it aloft as they watched the black-and-white television. Bruce was jumping up and down in excitement. However, at the moment, Rose came over pale. She went to the toilet and she found blood on her underwear, her baby miscarried. They both took this hard; it sent Rose into a deep depression. Nobody had warned her that this could happen. People had informed her about everything else, but this was a bastion that had not been breached, and her lack of understanding took the confidence from her. A gap opened between Rose and Bruce and a year later, he left.

At the age of twenty five Rose found some new fortune. She had moved away from London. A job took her to Thetford in Norfolk. It was there that luck pushed Lionel her way. He was an American serviceman working in logistics for the United States Air Force. They came together in a pub in Brandon, one chilly night, when they were sheltering from the cold. A year later they were married and Rose was on her way to Guam - Andersen Air Force Base. She learned about the Commissary, and the PX, where she shopped with US dollars. She learned how the other wives did their hair and make-up. She tried very hard to mimic their accents, but there was always a bit of East End of London on the middle of her tongue. She learned of the Fourth of July, and she sang the Star-Spangled-Banner, and she became an American. Then she became pregnant and this time there was no tragedy, Rose and Lionel's baby, Helen, was born, beautiful and healthy.

Then, one day, Rose learned that Lionel would not be coming home from the Vietnam War, he had been killed. Rose was in the States when the news came. Lionel's family were beside themselves with grief. Rose nursed her baby and cried, and she cried. Her baby, Helen, never knew her father, just as Rose had never known hers. It was later revealed that Lionel's death was caused by 'friendly fire'. 'Is that what they call it?' Thought Rose.

Helen's circumstances, materially, were somewhat better than the early years of Rose's life. There was food, there was warmth, and of course Lionel's family were Rose's family, and Helen was secure and safe from the things Rose had had to do to survive before she got to Nut Tree House.

The years ran on and Helen grew into an All American Girl. On sixth of September nineteen-ninety, Helen was in the Boardwalk Hall in Atlantic City for Miss America. Rose told her: "You could have been a contestant and won. Still it is wonderful you have such a great job as an assistant to Gary Collins, the presenter of the show, and you, only just coming on nineteen. I bet your dad is looking down from heaven right now so proud I'll bet he just fell of his cloud."

It was at this gathering that Rose met Peter, who worked for the NBC network, he was a television cameraman. Rose had to admit it was mostly the way Peter looked. He had the same posture as Lionel and there was something in his eye which was wild and exciting. Rose was forty-six years old, already.

The following year Rose and Peter were married. Kristopher's father had become a vicar, he and his wife had stopped working in childcare. Rose and Peter paid for him to fly from England to San Francisco to officiate at the wedding. What a wedding it was! Out in the open on a sun-drenched day, in the back yard of Peter and Rose's beautiful home. In the distance, as a backdrop, was The Oakland Bay Bridge which crossed San Francisco Bay. The band played the song, written by *George Cory* and *Douglass Cross,* which *Tony Bennett* recorded it in nineteen sixty-two, as a 'B Side' to the record 'Once Upon A Time', the Radio DJ's preferred the flip-side, and so it became famous; *'I Left My Heart In San Francisco'.*

During the wedding breakfast speeches Peter said.: "Rose and I have a special gift to give to Godfrey who came all this way from England to marry us today. We have made this book for you Godfrey, a scrapbook of Rose's life. Including some photos of you and your wife, June, all those years ago at Nut Tree House on The Rose Tree Estate. Rose asked me to do this because she said she would not be able to do it without crying. She has written at the beginning of the book 'To Godfrey and June. If you had not loved me I could not have loved Bruce, or Lionel, or Helen, and could not love Peter. So I thank you with all my heart for telling me, all those years ago, that the doors were not locked, but if I stayed you would care for me. I know I pushed all the boundaries; I was just trying to see if you really did care, you did, and so I am here. There are no thanks in the world enough to express what you did for me, and the other girls, over thirty years ago'."

Rose had experienced two more heartbreaks when Helen died of Cancer and Peter died in a road accident.

Rose wrote to Godfrey and to June regularly, she visited England on one occasion, shortly after Godfrey's death, and she visited June who was in a care home, a year after that. Rose wrote to June until June passed away. Then she wrote to Kristopher.

Chapter 16
Session Seven: Grandparents from Uganda
Kristopher

"The visit by grandparents from Uganda was a very special event. My grandparents were overjoyed to meet their two grandchildren. My dad, mum and I drove to the docks to meet them. My dad parked his car right by the ship. My grandparents disembarked and we met them on the quay. That is not a thing that is now possible.

My grandfather had asked my dad to purchase for him a new car. It was pale yellow. We drove in this car all the way to Torquay to see my grandfather's brother, William. That was a long journey. Back then, the main roads were punctuated by towns and traffic moved slower. We made a holiday there. My parents, Owen (my brother) and I, stayed with my grandfather's sister and her husband. They were called David and Iris. David worked for a bank and they lived in the apartment above it. After that trip my dad and grandparents travelled to Paris, they stayed there for a week, leaving the rest of us at Nut Tree House.

The strongest memory I have of the Ugandan visitation was not the cigarettes in yellow tin boxes that my Grandmother smoked. It was the day I sat next to her whilst we ate lunch. The pudding was banana custard. Bananas have a small stalk at one end. She found one in her mouth she spat it onto her spoon and then put it on the side of my plate. I scooped it up onto my spoon and started the spoons journey to my mouth. She reached out and slapped me on the hand and she said; 'You could die of that!' It was a shock. I cried. Nobody but me remembered this story. So I wonder have I made all this up, parking by the ship, the pale yellow car. No! There are some cine films of meeting my grandparents on the docks and there are one or two photographs that somebody took during that time. Funny thing about that is that the things in the films I have little memory of doing, the world beyond the films is so vivid I could touch it. I think I am repeating myself.

There was another memory of this banana incident. Grandmother, as she hit my hand, said a word I had not heard before - Ackee. She used this word whenever something was not good. Many years later I heard the words Akee Rice. It was in a song. *'Down the way where the nights are gay.......Akee Rice Salt Fish are nice. 'Jamaica Farewell'*...So I looked it up and found that

Ackee is a fruit. Ripe *'Blighuia Sapida'* properly cooked, and prepared, is considered delicious. If picked before they are ripe, and have grown to be open, they are toxic and can cause death if eaten. They sell them in tins soaked in brine." The fourteenth hour of deliberations with Doctor Samuels had sped by at a remarkable pace, when he told me my time was up my mind was still firmly fixed in nineteen fifty-nine.

Chapter 17
Pamela and Marcel
Narrator

For expedience, we will skip over Kristopher's eighth session with Doctor Samuels. I need to remind you of Pamela and Marcel. Pamela worked in the laundry on The Rose Tree Estate, around nineteen fifty-eight. Marcel was a French sailor, who had a relationship with Pamela. Pamela had put on a lot of weight and Marcel found her increasingly unattractive, but she was still useful to him.

Whilst Kristopher's grandparents were staying, the annual summer event occurred. The Sports-Day. All the house-parents, children of all ages, everyone came, including the cleaners, the office staff, and those who worked in the laundry, including Pamela and Marcel. Marcel found the whole idea of The Rose Tree Estate fascinating. His own childhood had been spent in a children's home in France. The beginning of his life had been very tough. He had been preyed upon by a man he had gone to live with after is mother and father had died. To the world, the man and his wife were like saints. At night Marcel found he was in the house of the Devil. In World War Two, Marcel served in the French Navy. He liked the life of a seaman, there were plenty of far off destinations where his face was just one of many that would come and go and that made satisfying his craving all the easier. Marcel would have sex with anyone, man or woman, and the younger the better.

The sports day was a wonderful success The Rose Tree Estate brass band led a procession to the sports field. There were running races for girls and boys split into different age groups. There was a proper starting gun which was very loud. The house-parents had their race and Mrs. Jefferson's husband came first. Then there were the silly races. Egg and Spoon', Three Legged, The Sack Race, and the funniest, The Blindfold Race. There were some serious athletes amongst the children. Some threw the javelin; there was long jump and high jump. After all the competitions, Kristopher's mum invited all to a feast, which had been prepared by a large cohort of women, she had led. It was a most magnificent buffet. There were sausage rolls and sandwiches. Pies and bread rolls with butter, soup, cakes and ice cream. The ice cream tasted better back then. Kristopher's mum had the knack of making everything look both professionally made and homemade all at the same time. Then a huge bonfire was lit and all sat about it singing jamboree Songs. She'll be coming round the mountain, Waltzin' Madelia, When the Saints, The crowds thinned as the younger folk went off to bed and, by eleven p.m., all that that remained of the day were the embers of the bonfire that had been so warming a couple of hours before.

Little Davy MacClue had not had much of a time since he ended up on The Rose Tree Estate, but today had been good. His little seven-year-old head fell onto the feather pillow. He had not wanted to end up on his own and such a great big world, but he was only one of many tiny people who had nowhere else to go. Tonight he disappeared into his dreams immediately. It was the first time that had happened. It was the sports day that did it.

It is very different belonging to something, which you have chosen to belong to, than it is to belong to something that has had to choose you for want of alternative.

Pamela had been working at The Rose Tree Estate laundry for a while. She invited Marcel to come to the sports day. He came in the hope of indulging in some sexual activity with Pamela, and maybe, others. The prospect was so enticing for him he could not refuse the invitation. Little Davy was unknown to Marcel, so Little Davy was spared the indignity of a sexual encounter at the age of seven years; another young boy was not as fortunate. More of that will be told later in this story.

Chapter 18
Session Nine: Polio
Kristopher

Growing in the lawn, in front of Nut Tree House, were two Monkey Puzzle trees. At Christmas time the trees were decorated with coloured lights. A display cabinet with a glass front was erected by the lawn, and in it, there was a scene of the Christian story of the birth of Jesus Christ. It included figurines and straw, after dark it was lit with an electric light. I have seen cine film of me in a brown one-piece, hooded suit, with wellingtons, in the snow at the front of Nut Tree House, pushing a wooden bat through the snow on the ground. I remember being dressed in a blue hooded jacket, ready for a journey to visit my granny's house by steam train, I went out and it had started to snow, I started to mess around outside and managed to get my nice clean clothes a bit muddy. I remember my mum being more than exasperated by this. She was really quiet cross!"

"There was a kind of sluice room for washing clothes and stuff. Maybe some things were stored in this room as I remember tins of baby milk powder on the shelf high up. I remember they were red tins, round with a baby's face on them, maybe the baby had a crown on his head. I remember too, glass pots of baby food. I remember these products being advertised on the television with the word NEW assigned to them, they still used the word NEW when my own children needed this kind of thing thirty years later!"

"The television was a new thing and I remember watching it in the evenings with the girls and my mum. In the daytime there was nothing on except the Test Card, or the Potters Wheel. At some stage they broadcast programmes for schools, but I am not sure if that was then. At lunchtime there was Watch With Mother although I always watched alone. It was often when these programmes came on that I needed to go to the toilet. I had the notion that if I switched the television off -- the programme would still be available when I returned! Of course you can do that today, but back then there was no way possible.

The bathroom holds memories of my dad making rabbit shadows withhis hands on the wall each evening at bathtime. He said that in the Boy Scouts, everyone was encouraged to take a bath every day. So we did. Looking back that was a big privilege then. Many people did not have indoor plumbing, indeed at the back of Nut Tree House were a row of outside toilets, although they were unused whilst I was living there, for bathrooms were put into the house. Many of the girls who were cared for, by my parents, would never have seen such luxury in other places in which they had lived."

"Other random memories would be of seeing the effects of letting off a fire-extinguisher in a corridor where there had been no fire! A man, who was a father of one of the girls, pulling a huge roll of bank notes from his pocket. The vending machine up the road, which would deliver a ball of chewing gum if a penny was inserted and a knob turned, oh, I mentioned that before, my aunt saw a boy spit into it. I remember too, many visitors to Nut Tree House. One woman came in a posh car, chauffer-driven; there was a glass partition between the driver and the back seat. Whilst the posh lady conversed with my parents, the chauffer would let me sit on his lap and I would steer the car as he operated the pedals and the gears to make the car move. This chauffer was a nice and clever man; he had magical powers and could produce a penny from behind my ear! The coin would then be given to me and I could, and I would, spend that money in the sweet shop. I remember being taken to the barbershop, watching the barber sharpening his razor on a leather strap. He put a padded shelf across the armrests of the barber chair and sat me on it, so that I was higher up than if I had sat down on the chair. It made it easier for him to cut my hair and I could see in the mirror. Once he had cut my hair he would show me the back of my head using a mirror to reflect into the mirror which was in front of me. He introduced me to white creem, which men put it in their hair to make it shine and keep it in place, something that was acceptable to my parents. Sitting in the barber's, waiting my turn, was the first time I heard the expression 'Something for the weekend Sir?' I did not know what that meant until a few years later when I went to primary school."

"There were two front doors at Nut Tree House, you could open the doors and venture down a short flight of concrete steps with a metal door-mat at the bottom alongside a boot scraper. In the earth beside these steps grew beautiful Flag Iris, one of my favourite flowers to this day. My brother, Owen, must have got to a stage in his life where he could walk. My dad was often keen for Owen and I to jump from the top of the stairs into his arms. I think Owen must have misjudged the situation, for one day he jumped but dad had his back turned. It was a catastrophe, Owen cut his forehead open and they rushed to the hospital where Owen had to have stitches to repair the wound."

"The Ford Anglia that my dad purchased was Black. After he bought it, he took granny, granddad and I out for a ride, all the way to Tunbridge Wells. We went to the Pantiles and drank from the spring. I do not think that the water tasted that good, but there was some orange squash which was added to make it bearable."

"For a special treat my dad would take me to an amusement park. It was something of a permanent funfair. There were electric cars to drive around a track and rowing boats to paddle up a water way surrounded by trees."

"Another outing took the whole family to some beautiful gardens which were open to the public. There was a horse trough there, still with water in it. There were still people who used horses for business, draymen still delivered beer on a flat bed wagon, and there were rag-and-bone men, who collected things people no longer used. These gardens were beautiful."

"My other memories include my mum hanging washing on the line and Owen, now able to toddle about, and I, sitting in washing-up bowls in the back yard, with water slopping about. Me climbing a step ladder to try and reach a rope that was on a hook."

"The sun shining in the windows of my dad and mum's bedroom, breakfast in bed, with toast in the toast rack."

"I was one of the lucky people to be given the polio vaccine, on a sugar lump, I knew people, later on, the same age as me who suffered this awful malady. It was a fine spring evening, when the doctor had finished feeding all the girls the magic potion we then all went for a walk down the neighbouring residential streets which were lined with blossom covered trees."

Chapter 19

What is a Nice Girl Like You Doing Here?

Narrator

"Amelia Pennywater, well that is a turn-up for the books! I wonder if life, down here, amongst the masses, will open her eyes?" Said Glenda, Matron of Spruce House, on The Rose Tree Estate.

"Why is she here?" Asked Noah Haddad.

Glenda answered: "It is very sad really. Amelia's Father, Theodore Pennywater."

"What that man who does all that posh horse riding? The black top-hat, jumping over gates and all. I saw him on the television only yesterday." Said Noah.

"Yes him, he his away in Dubai, or some such place. In the meantime Amelia was being cared for by a Nanny. Yesterday the nanny was in an accident and is in the hospital. Apparently the other staff are away and Amelia, although fifteen, is of course, not yet an adult. So she will be slumming it with our lot for a week until her father returns." Glenda said, followed by a shrug of her shoulders. She often did that as an expression of not being able to understand why, on Earth, had something happened. Many things did happen in Spruce House; but let us not get sidelined.

Noah then said. "Well she has caught the eye of a couple of the boys from Hornbeam House. I can't see that ending well. Anderson will have no flirtations from any boy in his crew."

"Mister Anderson to the likes of you Noah, thank you." Reprimanded Glenda. Just at that moment Beatrice Lampkins arrived for her all-night-shift at Spruce House.

"You'll be away and aft to yur bed the noo, leaving it up to the real workers, and yu noa, yu'll tak a lang-lie com the morn, fur it'll be yu day aft." Beatrice was from a wee village in Scotland, that na-bady in England had ever heard of, but she never left her voice behind, no matter how much her colleagues ribbed her. "Yu'd never ken what I just saw, wi ma own ee, that bonnie new lassie, Amelia, the wee one who turned up in riding jompers. Arh poor wee hen, the other lassies did whreek it oot o her. Weel I just seen hur stoatin aboot the wood, ourer there, we that loon fre Hornbeam hus. Now I cane see that endin weal if that Anderson finds oot."

Amelia, had fallen through her own looking glass twenty four hours before, when a social worker had taken her to The Rose Tree Estate in a car her father would never have given to a boot-boy. Amelia was perfectly sure she had seen a white rabbit. After she had eaten the food that they had presented at dinner the previous night, he could not face breakfast. For all that, she was in an intriguing situation. The like of which, in all her nearly sixteen -- it was just another month until her birthday -- she had never experienced before.

When she thought this, her mother's face came into her mind and a tear came to her eye. She knew her mother wanted to be with her on that special day, but her mother had been *lymphoma-ed* away. Her only siblings were the girls at her boarding school and on the face of it, The Rose Tree Estate and her school had much in common, except her father paid for her to be at that grand school. How much did that cost each year? She had overheard him one day, was it seven thousand a year plus the extras?!

The other very interesting thing was that here, unlike school, on The Rose Tree Estate, there were boys. No boy could get within a couple of miles of Brodway Hall where all the girls were nice young ladies, especially nice in summer all togged out in their straw-boaters and gingham. Amelia was aware of boys but there had not been many that she had been able to look over and assess. Now she found a whole house of them, more or less next door! Not only that they look clean and smart. They were also very polite. Within forty-eight hours the genes she had, had found some genes that were very opposite to her own; in a tall young man, about her age, from Hornbeam House. She noticed a little bit of stubble on his chin, although she was not aware that it was the nineteenth day of her menstrual cycle, her hormones were fully aware. Before anybody had noticed Amelia and Gary Watson had found the gardener's potting shed. It was warm, and there were some earthy smells, geranium and tomato. Amelia was not afraid; she learned not to be eight years before, a couple of months into the first term of boarding school. She had wondered, back then, how those Indian men walk on hot coals or lay on a bed of nails, then she went to boarding school and she found out how to survive. She learned to ignore the pain, and brutality of some of the older girls. She learned how to cope with the nasty comments some made, and the lies. Her dad paid a lot of money for her to learn such things. She also found that one of the teachers at Brodway Hall was known for being very interested in the games changing rooms. He would often walk in without knocking, just as the girls were about to shower after a netball match. On The Rose Tree Estate such education was often available for free. Gary Watson had learned much at Hornbeam House. It was a strict and fearsome place, but here he was, to his great surprise, with a gorgeous young female and he could not believe his luck. Amelia said, "What are you doing?"

Gary said: "It's alright, it will be nice." Her pants were on the potting shed floor; they caught a dried leaf or two. Gary was right; it was nice, she liked the feeling that Gary was a part of her. She felt her breath and held him and they both shuddered. It was a moment later that Amelia was pregnant with Gary's first child.

It took a little while for anyone to notice, but the consequences of sex with Gary in The Rose Tree Estate potting shed were far-reaching. Gary was summoned by Anderson, who only knew that Watson had been seen leaving the shed with the new girl. That was enough for Anderson to give Gary six strokes of the cane across his buttocks, in the night, when the other boys were in their beds. Amelia's Nanny noticed the pregnancy first, and when Theodore Pennywater found out, he was sure that his daughter had been raped on The Rose Tree Estate. He wanted to scream and shout and bring the culprit to justice; but there was no culprit, and how would it impact on his public image? Theodore had money and the privilege of friends who had their practices in Harley Street in London. Although abortion was illegal at that time, everyone kept very quiet. Only a handful of people ever knew. Gary certainly knew not. Amelia she knew everything, she knew the wonderful experience that she truly enjoyed with Gary. She also felt the searing pain of abortion. She saw her nanny's concern. She knew her fathers rage. She carried the pain of having her baby removed from her for the rest of her days.

Chapter 20
The Smell of Burning Hair
Narrator

Nina's father was from Jamaica. The *Windrush* bought him to the grey and drab place where he was to raise a family. Far from sunshine and calypso. The music he ended up conducting was the ding, ding of the bell on the bus as he shouted, "Any more fares please?" on the 109 bus to Westminster. He had rich, dark, brown skin. Nina's mother was from Brixton, she had never even had a suntan, she was always pale white. Having a child with a black man, was considered at that time, by some people, as very unhealthy. It was difficult, but she loved him. They made it work. Then there was a terrible fire, both her parents were killed in the blaze and Nina had had her face severely burnt, on the right side, and she lost her ear. She was very bitter, about it. She had had her family taken from her by the flames. She had no kin now and many people were cruel over mixed race parenting in those days. Nina became very hard. She could be violent, and she was very strong. She hated the way she looked, and, most of all, she hated her hair, which was always short, and always curly. She spent hours heating a hot metal comb on a small electric stove. With Vaseline and brown paper, and the dangerously hot metal comb, she would try to straighten it out. She would burn herself and other girls would try to help her. The atmosphere would become tense, and the air would fill with the smell of singed hair, and the others would complain.

Nina spent so much of her time defending herself it was hard for her to do anything else.

One sunny evening, after there had been a rounders match on the sports field, one of the house-parents came along with a trolley full of drinks, soup, and sandwiches. Nina pushed to the front and the house-parent gave her a reprimand. Nina picked up the large jug of soup and was about to bring it down on the head of the house-parent, when another house-parent leaped across the grass and rugby-tackled Nina to the floor. All the other rounders players scattered, the soup went up in the air in the jug and then fell to the ground. The jug broke into two equal parts, and the soup soaked into the grass. Nina lay on the ground for a moment, then she grabbed the arm of the rugby tackling house-parent and she bit into it with her teeth until she drew blood. The house-parent let out a banshee-like scream; Nina got up and fled from the scene. She ran from The Rose Tree Estate through the gates and down the road to the police telephone box. She told the police that she had been assaulted.

Chapter 21
Back to the Sports Day
Narrator

Now we return to the end of chapter seventeen.

Barbara was only twelve years old. She knew Pamela, because Pamela worked in the laundry of The Rose Tree Estate. So when Pamela told Barbara the there was a surprise waiting for her and she should come along quickly, the excitement was almost too much for Barbara. The surprise, Pamela assured her, would be a nice surprise. Barbara skipped along beside Pamela, innocent and unsuspecting. Pamela led Barbara to the back of the garden, away from the sports day, amongst the vegetables, and to the small wood near the greenhouse. Pamela told Barbara, that this was their secret, and she warned Barbara of the consequences of failing to keep a secret. Soon Barbara was so confused by the excitement of a surprise and the worry that she might not be able to keep the secret, she hardly understood as Marcel touched her. After it was over, Pamela gave Barbara a bag of jelly babies. She said;

"There you are Barbara your surprise." Then Pamela reminded her again that the special secret things that had happened must always be a secret, or the bogie-man would surely come. Barbara never felt the same about herself, The Rose Tree Estate, Pamela, or this man, who spoke in funny words, who had touched her where no one had touched her before. She felt guilt and she felt unclean. She threw the jelly babies, in their white paper bag, into the bushes, she ran to Hazel House, Pamela's words stinging her ears, 'Never tell George Gabon, or the bogie man will surely have you in the night'. She ran to the bathroom and she put the bath plug into the plughole, she turned on the taps and filled the tub. She took off her clothes, climbed into the warm water and scrubbed herself with soap. It was special, they called it toilet soap, she had seen the advertisement on the television, the friend whispering to a friend B.O.', she could smell Pamela's friend on her body, she could still feel his hands between her legs, she could smell him on her hand where he had made her rub him. She scrubbed between her legs until she was nearly sore. She wondered if the smell would ever go away, or if she would ever be able to think about anything but what had just happened ever again. She washed her face again and again, but even though the water she washed with was wet, it was not as wet as the tears she could not stop rolling down her cheeks. Her eyes were red.

Chapter 22

Session Nine: Granny's House

Kristopher

"One day my dad took me to see my granny. The drive took two hours. At last the road came to the countryside and we were half way there. I remember a petrol station, it had once been a barn, it was the kind of place that can be seen in old movies, it was quiet. Only my dad for a customer. The owner of the garage putting down a spanner and wiping his hands on an oily rag, filling the tank whilst my dad looked on. Once at my granny's house I had it in mind that I might stay with her a while. I put my little red wellingtons under the bed in the little room and announced my intention. The idea was accepted and I stayed."

"Many times I stayed with my granny and granddad. It was a terraced house with gardens front and rear. The front garden had a patch of grass with flower borders, which were home to antirrhinums; to the left there was a concrete path to the front door. The door was wooden with glass lights in the top. Immediately inside the front door was the staircase to the left. The front room to the right. Further in was the kitchen and the main living room to the right. Upstairs were two bedrooms with double beds, and a single bedroom and bathroom."

"There was a long garden to the rear with allotments beyond the fence. The garden contained a washing line, fruit trees, a vegetable patch, and flower borders."

"The day with Granny had a rhythm. It began with the twilight of dawn. I would leave my bed and push up under the covers of my grandparents bed and squeeze between them staring up at the ceiling which had cracks in the plaster. These straight lines could turn into aeroplanes with propellers, or roads with dead ends. There were similar cracks in the windowpanes; the lines were rounded, like the crows feet that can appear by the eyes of people as they age. The automatic tea-maker would start to gurgle and hiss until at last the scalding, boiling, water would gush out of the spout and in to the tea pot. Hissing and wissing only inches from my granny's head. As the last drops shushed on to the tea, granddad would climb, wearily, from the bed and organise the cups of tea for granny and him. He never said a word. He squeezed granny's cup onto the table, by the bed, on which stood the automatic tea-maker. She would be still lying under the sheet, which was always pulled up right over her face. Granddad would disappear into the bathroom and he would break wind twice. Then he shaved and did his other ablutions, before coming back into the bedroom to pull on his long johns and dress for work. He would go downstairs for his breakfast, by which time the morning paper would be in the letterbox. Then, at the same time every day, he climbed the stairs and said goodbye to granny, she would pull the sheet from her face, he would kiss her on the head and say.

'See you at lunch time.'

"He left the papers on the bed and granny would sit up and drink her tea. Then she would read the papers. One of the papers had a cartoon of a bear and she would read the captions to me. She glanced through the news, then she would tackle 'The Word'. This was a game, a printed square divided into squares, with a black column to the right containing one white capital letter. To the left nine other letters in nine white boxes with black letters printed in them. The idea was to make as many words as possible from the available letters, every word had to contain the white letter, all the words had to be three letters or more. It was always possible to make one word by using all ten letters. Granny loved this and she was very good at it. She checked her score daily, so as not to lower her average."

"The next thing was to get dressed. It may have been for the cold, or it may have been because I was there and so to avoid embarrassment, granny would get dressed in bed. The covers would fly. She wore a roll-on girdle to keep her tummy flat, stockings could be suspended from it, she would tell me she had the figure of a model. Once the elaborate spectacle was at an end, we would go down the stairs to light the fire. The house had a small paraffin heater upstairs for the really cold nights. Downstairs, in the living room was a coal fire. This was all the heating for the whole house. First, the ashes had to be removed and put out on the garden. Then a mix of newspaper, kindling and coal was set in the grate, this was totally different from my dad's method. Once the fire was alight, granny made busy in the kitchen, she prepared my breakfast, a second cup of tea for herself and her food drink. She would complain about not sleeping. She wore earplugs to shut of the sound of granddad's snoring. She took sleeping pills, which she claimed never worked."

"The wireless would be on, (N.B. Younger readers, this was not WiFi wireless, I am writing of radio) not all the time, but when she could she liked to keep up with *'Mrs. Dales Diary'*. She would set to with the household chores, cleaning this and that. I would do the dusting. She washed the sheets in the sink, by hand, and hung them out to dry. Folding them carefully, she laid the dry sheets under the foot end of her bed's mattress in some attempt to press them. When ironing had to be done, the electric light, in the living room ceiling was where the iron was plugged in. There was a double-socket, Bakelite adapter hanging from the wire attached to the ceiling rose. Thinking of that now is a bit frightening, for the cables of an electric lighting circuit are designed to carry much less current than the ring main. Or maybe it was all the same back then. Looking back it is a wonder that the place failed to catch fire."

"Granddad did say he would have liked to have been an electrician. I remember some years later he did re-wire that house and after that, the electric sockets upstairs were switched on by the light switches downstairs!"

"Granddad worked in a coach building factory. He was a foreman. He made the doors for the coaches. Before that he had built wooden chassis for Rolls Royce cars. Before that he was an apprentice carpenter. He could really turn his hand to any carpentry or metalwork. Laminating with a heat-resistant wipe clean plastic, was 'the thing' at that time, and he covered the dining table and all the windowsills with it. When I was a bit older he made me the best go-cart ever. The old cupboard, which granny had used for her shoes, was secured to a plank of wood. One of the doors was removed so I had a cockpit. Wheels from an old pram were fixed below the plank and, on a hot summer's day, Granddad lit the living room fire and heated the biggest soldering iron most people would ever have ever seen. After a long time roasting in the flames, it was hot enough to melt a huge blob of solder on an old fire poker which he then used to attach wheels to the axel at the front of the cart. The smell of the flux, and the heat of the iron were extraordinary. The cart had a steering stick, like they had in an aeroplane. The wonderful vehicle was painted purple, and Granddad painted *Z Victor II* on the back. So it was now a police car from *Z-Cars*, a famous television show from the BBC, it ran from nineteen sixty-two to nineteen seventy-eight. I kept every possession I had in the boot of my go-cart. My pals and I had a brilliant time with it. Then some evil person stole it and I never saw it, or my possessions again."

"Getting back to the story, and the routine with granny. When breakfast over and the fire was alight, there were always other cores. The washing-up, I had to dry. There were occasions when, as a treat, I would be allowed to have a soap filled scouring-pad so that I could stand at the sink and scrub all the pots and pans until they were shining like a new sixpence. We would prepare food, shelling peas, cutting runner beans and peeling the potatoes. Then there were the shops to visit. Sometimes my aunty Susan, who lived opposite granny, would come too. It was not far to go; a short walk up the hill past the pub. Once granddad took me to that pub, he left me outside in the car park whilst he went in. It was dark by the time he returned to me. In the twenty-first century there would surely have been complaint regarding the neglect of me. I suspect that granny never knew about that, I am sure she would not have been best pleased. It was not a very nice place to wait. Cars came and went, I could see shop windows that might have given me some interest but they were the other side of the busy road which I had been forbidden to cross on my own. The shops included: Co-Op, the greengrocer, the butcher and the dairy. Sometimes, if I was lucky, we would go to the sweet shop and buy Granny's favourites (there were many) Barley Sugar, Hard Gums, Sugar Coated Almonds,

Mints, or Chewy Fruits. I would settle for a mixed bag of penny sweets, Sherbet Saucers, Shrimps, Red Liquorice, Chocolate Bananas, Fruit Gums. The chemist was another stop. Aunty Susan was very keen on orange vitamin C tablets, she was convinced that we would never get a cold if we took one every day. She would often top-up this dose of vitamin with concentrated orange squash and rosehip syrup. Granny would buy *eau de cologne,* and smelling salts. The newsagent's was next door to the chemist, and when the papers had to be paid for, the women, behind the counter had a large black folder with very important looking papers in it. She quizzed the pages and relayed the cost, granny passed over her money and the debt was scored from the pages. Sometimes we would wait in line for the Post Office, it was at the back of the newsagent's shop. I liked waiting in the queue because there were a good number of toys to look at in this part of the shop.

Most things that could be needed were available from these shops.

The butcher's had sawdust on the floor, great if we were there early and I could make patterns in it with my feet. The baker's had the best farmhouse loafs of bread, and milk and cheese was in plentiful supply from the dairy. Oh how I crave that bread whenever I enter a baker's these days, only to be disappointed by the lack of whatever magic made that bread so fantastic. Oh, and milk where the cream floated to the top."

"The shopping area had four parts, the last bit had the bank and the Fish and Chip shop, which sometimes, at night, my granddad and I would go to get our supper, the smell was always enticing. The bundle would be wrapped in newspaper, and we would take the feast back to granny. Sometimes, on a Sunday, granddad would buy a special treat of ice cream. That to was also wrapped in newspaper in an attempt to insulate it from the warmth. Granddad would put it in the front room, in the shade, until it was pudding time. They had no fridge.

"Granny would serve such good food; mashed bananas with top of the milk and sugar; chips fried in butter in the frying pan; fried eggs; mince and potatoes; porridge oats prepared with top of the milk and sugar; custard and often we enjoyed instant coffee. Roasted chicken was a rare, and special, thing then. We toasted crumpets on a fork by the fire. Sometimes potatoes wrapped in foil were pushed into the fire and left for the day to be eaten in the evening.

"When I was with granny was not alone, as I so often was at Nut Tree House. At granny's house I would go into the garden but she often looked out of the window or door to check on me. It seems to me that some of the best days of my childhood were spent with granny and granddad. I think too that even though I was not their child, they loved me as if I was. Of course, as I so often state, there were things that were okay then, but considered now, would be regarded as being incorrect. For example, each evening granny, granddad and I would sit by the fire, the television would be on, I would be drawing, or playing with some toys, or something. Granddad would read his newspapers, catching up with granny. Whilst he read he would smoke his cigarettes, but we knew no better then. Granddad smoked so much he was able to collect hundreds of coupons from the cigarette packets. One day we took the bus into Brighton, we went to the arcade and into the *Cigarette Catalogue Shop* it was more than just a ground floor. With the coupons for payment, I was able to obtain several toy cars, and fine they were. I have never been a smoker so the advertising ploy did not work on me, but I am sure that it must have worked on others."

"Sometimes I would go over to play at aunty Susan's house in the morning. Granddad would come home from work for his lunch. He would collect me and we would cross the road to his house to eat."

"There were many fun things to do with aunty Susan, my cousin, Sharon, the same age as me, she had many toys, and was always a lot of fun."

"When lunch had been eaten, granddad would leave to catch the bus back to work, sometimes he walked. I am sure he was a good worker. I remember that one Saturday morning he took me to the factory to see what went on there. It was a dark place, for the main part, I saw furnaces where metal was made red-hot so that it could be shaped. There were huge machines and much noise. Granddad knew everyone and they knew him. Granny told me that once there had been a strike of the workers, but granddad refused to stop work. All the other men ganged up against him and Sent him to Coventry, which meant they would not talk to him for many months."

"I think from all that you can understand just how different my early life was from most of the youngsters on The Rose Tree Estate."

"Looking back the contrast between my privileged life and the lives of those my parents cared for, was like the desert and the ocean. I have no doubt I was loved, despite what I might have said about being left to get on with it. I was glad that they let me get on with it. The fact is, I had support in every direction. I always had food, clothes and toys. No one threatened to hit me, and nobody, I can remember as I speak, did harm to me. I suppose that is what this session has been all about. I suppose there is guilt within me, which knows just how lucky I was. Yet there I was alongside these people, whose lives had not started so well. I began my life so differently, yet we were in the same place, I was surely as vulnerable as they were had there been some pervert lurking. Or was I protected by who I was, rather than who the others were?"

Chapter 23
The Young Ones
Narrator

Wendy and Douglas were house-parents, in Laburnum House on The Rose Tree Estate. It seemed to all that knew them, that Wendy and Douglas had always worked at Rose Tree. Actually Wendy began her career as house-parent two years after Douglas, who had started his job in nineteen fifty-nine. Twenty-five years had disappeared by the time Douglas got around to proposing to Wendy, and in June nineteen eighty-four they had only been courting for a week. Douglas knew in nineteen sixty-one that Wendy was the girl for him. However, the idea of walking-out with a colleague was not an acceptable thing at the time. Wendy knew that Douglas was the man for her the first time she saw him. She wanted to say something, to give him a sign; she wanted him to know how she felt. It just was not what a nice girl would have done on The Rose Tree Estate back then. Of course these notions were not correct, if they had declared their undying love, no one would have been displeased, but there was a thought that said such an idea would be unacceptable.

Unacceptable things were going on all over The Rose Tree Estate, although Wendy and Douglas were not a party to any improper behaviour, they were alert to rumours and had decided to put up a united front to ensure that none who were in their care would ever come to harm. To that end they were a very successful team, as far as they knew.

On the nineteenth June, nineteen eighty-four, Wendy and Douglas were both on late duty and the young folk in their care were gathered about the Laburnum House television set. The BBC Two channel was broadcasting images of Rik, Nigel, Adrian and Alexei in the alternative comedy *The Young Ones.* It was the last episode of the series entitled *Summer Holiday.* The youngsters found the programme very funny, they laughed as Vivienne hit Neil with a cricket bat as he came from his bedroom which had been invaded by a family of strangers. Wendy and Douglas had discussed whether or not the programme was a suitable thing for the youngsters to be watching, but it would have been difficult to stop them, surprisingly, Douglas said,

"The children do not hit each other with cricket bats, even when they have watched the programme! I think it is safe enough."

Then Mr. Elephant-head appeared on the screen and Wendy and Douglas slipped into the corridor.

Wendy said. "I really cannot abide that programme, what do they see in it?"

Douglas then said something that he had only imagined saying a moment before. "Wendy I have known you for twenty five years, or thereabouts. That awful programme has just made me realise that the world has changed. Frankly I am still living in the nineteen-fifties, always avoiding asking you the question that I have wanted to ask you since nineteen sixty-one." He paused a moment and said: "Wendy could I take you out to dinner?"

Wendy said: "Yes".

Wendy and Douglas did not kiss, that was not the sort of thing that one would do whilst on duty. Wendy pushed open the door of the television room and Douglas and she saw a red *Route Master* London Bus, plunge down a cliff, smash down the side and explode at the bottom of a quarry, to the gleeful laughter of all the youngsters sitting about the television set.

"The world has changed Miss. Courtney. Many of us are tied up in what was, and what should be, we fail to notice things happening all about us," said Douglas to Wendy.

"Things have changed Mr. Morgan." Replied Wendy, "I am glad we are, at last, changing too. I have heard some stories, recently, which I find disturbing; I think we should discuss them later. There is a really nice restaurant in Katharine Street in town. Do you know it?"

A week later Douglas had proposed and a date was fixed for Wendy and Douglas's wedding.

What a wedding it was. All the children form all the homes on The Rose Tree Estate lined the main road through the estate and the band played. The wedding party was held on the lawn outside Nut Tree House. There was dancing and food and drink. The sun went down, and the bonfire was lit, fireworks ripped into the sky and whizzed and banged. No one who was there ever forgot that day.

Chapter 24
Mental Hospital
Narrator

It would have been good to have a golf buggy to move around this huge building, the main corridors were wide enough. Lino floors had been fitted to roll up the side of the walls a little way before being straighten off with an aluminium rod which was screwed on top of the lino to secure it to the wall. Above the aluminium there was a shiny eggshell coloured gloss paint which had been applied to about half way up the wall giving way to a magnolia emulsion which took this dazzling interior decoration to the ceiling. The ceiling was painted in a white emulsion. Now after years of neglect it was greying with age and there were mysterious yellow-brown sprayings at irregular intervals here and there. The monotony of the paintwork was broken by a red fire alarm button with 'break the glass' etched on it. Regularly there would be a set of wooden and glass doors, which are always held back by hooks.

These, forever, corridors were often decorated by various shades of the human form. Old men in hand-me-down suits, ill fitting and stained with whatever they had had for breakfast or an accident when he did not quite make it to the loo in time. There were women with handbags, full with the stuff they collected from around and about. Some made sure they picked up the leftovers from the last meal that had been provided for them, carefully wrapped in toilet paper, the old fashioned hard type, typical in institutions of then. Many of the old men would walk with their eyes pointed directly to the ground, scouring the lino for the 'dog ends' of already smoked cigarettes which had been snubbed out by other, more affluent and extravagant inmates. They collected the 'dog ends' and broke them open to collect any remaining tobacco, which they would then store in a small metal tin until they had collected enough to roll-up into a new cigarette from the nicotine soaked remnants. Occasionally someone would pass by with a bottle of mentholated spirits, partly concealed in a brown paper bag. Mostly they drank that outside in the grounds of the hospital under the shade of the huge beech trees. Sometimes, at a turn in the path or in the alcove of a door frame, a couple of bodies would be locked in intercourse. She returning the favour of a real cigarette, which he had stolen, and given to her for this favour. Then there could be a crowd, the odour could be thick, and unwashed, and there, in the midst, a naked woman, a patient who had lost all her inhibitions, and in her frustration, had ripped off her clothes, and left them in a pile.

The corridors were the pathways to the wards of the hospital, some were open and patients were free to wander, others had double doors which were secured, at all times, to prevent the escape of those who would do harm to themselves and to others if they were given the chance. It was on one such ward that Sylvia lived her life. Her childhood had been spent on The Rose Tree Estate. The health of her mind had always been in doubt. Anyone on the estate, during the years Sylvia spent there, would have told you that Sylvia was loopy, mad, crazy, a nutcase. It was no wonder really, for her father had done unspeakable sexual things to her when she was only a few months old. Abuse had found its way to her often as she was growing up, so much so, that it was not so much abuse, it was just a way of life.

She was about twenty-one years old when she came to the hospital, and for many of the years she had lived there the medical staff had controlled her violent tendencies with drugs. She, and her ward mates, knew all the drugs, Lithium for depression. Chlorpromazine for the schizophrenics. Antipsychotics to manage psychosis. Most spent long periods of their time under the influence of these medicines. Their eyes hollowed and their skin grey. Sylvia lived in the hospital for thirty years, and she died there at the age of fifty-one.

Silvia was not the only person from The Rose Tree Estate who was committed to live in this asylum. There was Bill Doherty; he went missing from his ward. The police searched for him. They found him three months later. He was sitting in a chair, in a disused ward, which should have been locked. He had died there, in that chair, a sad end to a sad life.

They have demolished that hospital now and built a new housing estate in the grounds amongst the beech trees. I was there at the last part of the demolition. I peered over the fence at the piles of bricks. Surely those new houses will be haunted by the likes of Sylvia and Bill, whose only mistake was to have been born into sad circumstances, and who's lives were left unimproved by their stays at The Rose Tree Estate.

Chapter 25
Reynash
Narrator

There was a small Indian boy. His skin was covered in eczema. It caused him to scratch, and his skin would bleed. They cut his nails so he could not scratch. He was anaemic, so each day he was given foul tasting medicine of iron. The effect of this was to give him constipation. He would then be given laxatives and then he would have diarrhoea, which he was unable to control, and sometimes nursery nurses would become exasperated and annoyed that they had to clean the floor, or change his short trousers and underpants. Sometimes they would shout at him. Reyansh had become somewhat immune to this, and showed little response. They bathed him in slimy baths of *Betnovate*, and sometimes, at night, they would splint his arms with a stick across his back, his arms bandaged to it as Jesus on the cross, removing the slightest possibility of Reynash easing his discomfort by scratching his fiery, irritated skin. The nursery nurses followed the instructions of their elders and betters; never wincing at the tasks they were taught to perform. For they were told that this was the way to help and protect Reynash.

There were suggestions that the eczema, the dermatitis was caused by allergic reactions or house-dust mites. It was in a similar category to asthma. Many years after the experiences you have just read about, scientists discovered that asthmatic children were often cured by a *parentdectamy*, a phrase from a book by an American physiologist. Some asthmatic children, it seems, suffered their condition because they channelled the anxiety of their parent. Maybe the eczema suffered by Reynash was a product of his own anxiety. How would you feel so young, so alone, not understanding what these big people were doing? One minute cuddling and laughing, next minute, angry and cross and why do this to my arms? How would they feel not being able to scratch?

Reynash had a poor start on the road of his life, but when one of the nursery nurses gave up her job to marry a man from India, she and he adopted Reynash and his life in Willow House, on The Rose Tree Estate, came to a close. He had a new mother and father who truly loved the fragile little brown-skinned boy. It was only a short while and the eczema vanished and his skin became smooth and soft. His doting parents gave him foods that negated the necessity for iron supplements. He no longer needed *Senokot*, and he no longer suffered with diarrhoea.

Years went by and Reynash grew, he went to school and then to university where he studied law, making his parents proud. Reynash became a Lawyer. He bought his parents a house in the countryside, later he married and he and his wife adopted three Indian children.

You may recall at the start of this story Kristopher was in his tenth session with Doctor Samuels and he was remembering the first session.

Chapter 26

Session Ten: Incy-wincy Spider

(Continued from the start this story)

Kristopher

Granny told me that when she had been thirteen, granddad had put a note through her door asking her to go out with him. That would have been in nineteen-fourteen, the year that the First World War began. She said she was quite shocked and was not sure about the idea. He persisted and so finally she caved in. Just before they were married he asked if she would help him with his problem. Only once married did she find out what the problem was -- He liked to gamble."

"It was my granny who pushed and found them the house to buy on the new estate of houses. My mum would have been about four years old and her sister about two. They purchased the house for six hundred pounds. The children grew up there, and once they had grown, my mum moved away but Susan and her husband bought a house just over the road from granny and granddad's. Then, after a gamble too far, granddad gave the deeds of the house over on a bet that failed. Granny was mortified, she found out who had the deeds and went to them, she shouted and screamed, she ranted and raved, and finally they returned the deeds to her. In the bottom of her wardrobe she kept an old-fashioned doctors bag. A Gladstone Bag. It was kept locked. In it were all the important papers. When granddad came home from work on a Friday night he would hand over his unopened wage packet, granny opened it, she took out some of the money and gave it to granddad, some of the rest was put into granny's purse and the remainder went into the doctors bag. Granny kept an absolute grip on the finances. Even so, during one of my stays at their house, granddad went missing. He simply did not return from work: granny and aunty Susan were beside themselves with anxiety. Susan took to peering up and down the road, if she saw anyone looking like her father she would set off at a trot to see if it was him. The boss of the coach factory, where granddad worked, came to the house. I do not know how long granddad was away, I cannot remember, I do remember the fear in granny as she tried to keep her world together. Then, out of the blue, granddad returned. I was never privy to what had exactly happened. However, I did realise that awkward things can happen in any family. The families of the children who lived on The Rose Tree Estate, and my own, lucky family, were not that far apart. Why had granddad left and then come back? Was it more gambling? Or something else?"

"After lunch, each weekday at granny's house, the television provided *Watch with Mother. Andy Pandy, The Wooden Tops, Bill and Ben the Flower Pot Men. Picture Book.* That was at one-thirty, at one-forty-five it was *Listen with Mother* on the wireless. Granny would have finished cleaning up in the kitchen and would take up her chair by the fire. She would cover her head and eyes with a scarf, or her leather glove, and doze to the sound of the wireless. *Daphne Oxenford,* and a gentleman would sing a nursery rhyme then there would be a story followed by another nursery rhyme. *Polly put the Kettle on, Little Boy Blue, The Grand Old Duke of York, Hot Cross Buns, Simple Simon.* Television, later in the day, provided; *Captain Pugwash, Twizzel, Space Patrol* and a fairytale from some other country, often in a language other than English. Over the years there were many others. All the programmes were in black and white. Of an evening, granddad would often have fights with the vertical and horizontal holds as he clicked the knob around to change from BBC to ITV. He would unplug the set before we went to bed and watch as the little dot in the middle of the screen disappeared. Televisions were full of valves and they got very hot, television often caused fires, ensuring that granddad was cautious."

"At two o'clock it was *Woman's Hour.* When this was over it would be time for an outing. Maybe to see the pigs, or sometimes down to the beach. Sometimes to see one of granny's friends."

"We walked a lot, we also went on the buses a lot. If it rained, it rained, and we got wet, a lot! We walked through the snow and the sun. When the dandelions were yellow, the warning was that we would wet the bed if we touched them. When they had gone to seed we were told to pick them and blow the seeds away so we could tell the time. We picked blackberries in the late summer. It was as good as life could get."

"I loved to swim in the sea, sunshine or cloud, it mattered not to me. I had my goggles and diving into the grey waters of Hove beach, with it's huts, and The Westend Café was wonderful. Maybe it was those earlier experiences of all but drowning, I had conquered this swimming on my own, no help, no instruction, I just felt confident. The Westend Café provided toasted teacakes. Sometimes there were boats to be rowed on the lagoon, and ice cream cones called *'99',* a chocolate *flake* in Mr, Whippy, soft ice cream."

"Whatever the afternoon excitement, we had to return in time for granddads tea. It had to be prepared and put on the table. He had done a hard afternoon's work, so it was only right that granny made him the meal he needed to restore his strength."

"Early evenings in the summer might have seen us go out to the pictures, granny often took us to the pictures to see a *Disney* movie. *Snow White, The Sword in the Stone, The Jungle Book.* Or may be we would take the open top bus from Portslade to Rottingdean, the number 77."

We would watch the television, and after the *Nine o'clock News* we would climb the hill to Bedfordshire. The struggle at this point was to leave the warmth of the fire and go out into the freezing cold house. Why granddad bothered with the paraffin heater I did not know, it made little, or no, difference to the temperature. Still, we always had a milky bedtime drink before we went up the stairs, then, once under the sheets, blankets and the eiderdown, and with the hot-water bottle, it was soon warm enough. I would dream until morning. Oh! how I wish I could sleep the whole night now without having to get up to visit the bathroom, just like those days nearly sixty years ago."

"I remember not only all these things that happened but my dreams also. Some were recurring nightmares. My dad driving his car, he fainted, I reached over from the back seat to gab the wheel and steer us to safety. I climbed the ladder of a slide in the park, but as I got to the top, the ladder became detached from the slide and fell backwards -- it kept falling never hitting the ground. I dreamt I was on a swing, which was the seat in an helicopter, the fuel was coca-cola."

"As if those dreams were not enough, I also dreamed something that, if I had told anyone, would probably have caused alarm. I did not think of that then of course. It did not cause me alarm, yet it was strange. You may well think it strange. I wonder if you will dear doctor?"

"For I know now with breathtaking certainty, that this is what you have been searching my head for. You have found it doctor! The hairs on the back of my neck are tingling and I have goose-pimples all over my body. It is as if one of Death's bony hands has reached out from behind his black cloak and touched my shoulder, I caught a glimpse of his scythe."

Doctor Samuels was silent; he arched his fingers before his mouth and listened intently.

"Remember I was a very young child and consciously I had, I thought, never seen in real life, what I dreamed. Much later in my life I did think of these dreams, and I tried to understand what I had dreamed and how I could have dreamed them. I remember having a conversation with a doctor. I asked her if she thought that if we get so many physical traits from or parents, and often mental traits too, did she think it was possible that we could inherit some history too, maybe some deeply emotional moments are passed on at conception. The doctor's reply was to look astonished and then she said:

"What a fascinating notion, I have never thought of such an idea. I wonder if anyone has. Maybe there are some university guys in America who have studied such an idea. They get grants for the most extraordinary, bizarre, ideas over there. I cannot think in my own life that I have some of my father's or mother's memories, but I wonder how one could distinguish between the stories one has been told when young, and histories that have crossed the generations."

"Doctor Samuels. At three, four and five years old, I had never seen a person without their clothes; the only naked bodies I had seen belonged to me. The vision, of myself was that of looking down. I had seen my face in a mirror, but not the rest of me, for the mirror was hung too high, and the space in the bathroom was insufficient, I had to climb the bathroom stall just to look at my face. Apart from my own body the only other person I had seen naked was my brother, Owen, almost three years my junior. So the dream I had was strange. Stranger for I knew exactly what I was dreaming of, although why, and what the circumstances, within the dream were, I did not know. These things are nearly sixty years old and, as I speak, I am unable to understand the consequences of what I am about to reveal, the entirety of it all eludes me. As I tell you this, you should be aware that I am sure I have not been a victim, and I am sure I was not assaulted. However, I feel extraordinarily insecure as I speak these words -- there is something more that I need to grasp, and I cannot as yet."

The room went silent for more than a minute and then the doctor spoke.

"Kristopher I do not wish for you to be so distressed, it is ok, you have done really well. The cages you told me about in one of our early sessions, it appears that you have arrived at them."

The doctor ruffled through a wedge of papers as thick as a book. Then he said: "Yes I have your exact words, I noted them.

'I secured those thoughts in cages six decades ago. I was still fighting to keep you away from those cages; they are in the darkest corridor in my mind. They had been there for so long I had almost forgotten they were there. I do not remember what is in them, I just know doctor that they are full of things I never wanted to think of again. I can hear the sounds of these things, they are as ferocious beasts, screeching and roaring.'

"We, I think have, at last, come to the darkest corridor Kristopher. It is ok pause, you are safe here, no harm can befall you."

I could not look at the doctor; I fixed my mind on the imaginary grandfather clock, which should have been tick-tocking in this place. Then suddenly I blurted it out from my throat, where it had been stuck for nearly sixty years. I felt the words burning on my tongue like yellow bile when your stomach is empty, and there is no food to spew up. As the words escaped my lips, I wanted them to stop. It was too late, they hit the air beyond my face, and amplified into the twilight of the doctor's room. I have no concept of what the words meant, but I knew then, as I knew when I had been three, four and five years old, that the words were like the white foam on a wind-swept sea, and that the foam was only one small part of a wave, which would actually turn into a tsunami.

"The dream I had was of a fat, naked woman." I paused for breath. "It was a greenhouse. It was built from bricks about three feet from the ground up. Then a wooden frame, painted white, with a myriad of glass lights to let in the sun and keep out the cold. The smell about the greenhouse was peculiar to other greenhouses, I experienced later in my life. It was a smell that I found attractive. Huge hollyhocks grew beside a water butt which collected water from the roof when it rained. The gardener told me. There were other people involved, but what their involvement is not yet clear, or understandable to me. The dream involved me driving my tricycle along the road to one of the homes on The Rose Tree Estate.

"The water from the butt was much better because it was pure rain water with no chemicals, it was soft water, the water from the tap contains a lot of chalk which makes it hard, the gardener told me, he told me lots of things, he was kind to me."

"I feel as if I am in shock doctor, I am in over my head, and my understanding, but that gardener had been kind enough to talk to me, and put ideas in my head, and so as time went on and I learned things about water, the memory of that conversation returned. I could see this gentleman, who had such love for his flowers, and who gave me a lot of his time. I would run after him as he mowed the lawn. He would share his fruitcake with me, when he had his cup of tea in the morning. He told me the names of flowers, and let me hoe the weeds that had grown between the lettuces. In his potting shed he had a picture hanging on the wall of a woman wearing a girdle, like my granny wore.

In my dream of the fat naked lady, the gardener did not feature somehow, or another, she was in, and beside that green house.

In various versions, that dream repeated in my sleep many times.

Doctor Samuels closed this session with reassuring words and instructions to call immediately if the stress of these memories became too much to bear before our next appointment.

Chapter 27
Data Protection
Narrator

On the television news, one summer evening, it was reported, that in an old building, which the council were due to demolish, had been found to be full of council documents dating from the end of the Second World War through to the nineteen eighties. Much of the material was marked *confidential.*

Anthony Lockhart was the owner of the demolition firm. He had lived in, and grown up on, The Rose Tree Estate. It was he who went to reconnoitre the building and had used a crowbar to break off the padlock on the cellar door in which the 'treasure trove' was hidden, collecting dust and forgotten. He shone his torch about the room, it was a mess, old filing cabinets, broken wooden drawers. There were architect's drawings and medical reports. There was a cabinet clearly marked 'The Rose Tree Estate'. The lock was no match for the crowbar and soon Anthony was skimming through a file. There were names of children and staff, logs and accounts. It was all too much to read in a short period of time. So from the drawer, Anthony pulled out of the draw an arm full of files. He walked back up the stairs, secured the outer door and took the files to his home. That evening he read as much as he could. He found his name there and reports about him. There was a pencil-written note in a margin, which also appeared alongside many other children's names. PVOT. On the bottom of the first sheet upon which Anthony's name appeared was; PVOT = Possible Victim of Thacker. Anthony was transported back to his childhood and he knew that the word 'possible' should be erased.

Chapter 28
Session Eleven: Parent in Lieu
Kristopher

Doctor Samuels greeted me with extra fervour and a warm handshake. He reminded me that his secretary had telephoned me, twice, to ask of my well-being after the big reveal of the previous session. He asked me if I was alright and he invited me to continue my stories.

"The weekends were different of course, granddad had to work in the morning on Saturday but was free after lunch. Sometimes this meant a visit to Brighton and a walk down The Lanes. There was one shop, which I liked more than the others. It was a stationer, I always liked pencils, pens, paper and notebooks, I still do.

If we went somewhere on Sunday it was not to Church; instead we would visit the Palace Pier and the Volkes Railway. We would see many coaches parked up along the road to Black Rock.

"I could have rose-coloured spectacles, but I do not think so. I know that I was so fortunate to have my parents, they were people who really loved and cared for me -- and everyone else that they had to deal with. They were ordinary people, without wealth, but both with good self-esteem and self-control. The world, back then, was neater, and tidier, and much more cared for than the world in which I tell these memories today. The Automobile Association man, in his brown uniform would salute when he saw a car displaying an *AA* badge. The discipline of wartime still hung in the air and provided clear lines of respect between people. I feel most lucky that I had this start in life and that I can recall, in detail, so much of it."

"The landscape I have laid out above, of visits to granny and granddad, were over a good few years, at this time I was either pre-school age or attending primary school."

"How many people can speak good words about the memories of their childhoods? I do not know, but I still have more to say."

"I have remembered something which did frighten me. It was a conversation which I overheard when we were first at Nut Tree House. It was one of the house-parents explaining the use of that room I told you of. The large room that had the funny toilet in the middle. I remembered that there were lots of bikes in there. I remember hearing the house-parent tell my dad that when girls arrived at Nut Tree House, the first thing that would happen to them is that they would have to remove all their clothing and be showered. They were then obliged to use the toilet. The expression on my dad's face was grim. He then told the house-parent.

"Such practice will cease."

It was my dad who turned that room into a bike store.

"I will not allow such humiliating practices to occur to anyone that my wife and I care for." Was my dad's instruction.

The house-parent protested, saying:

"You must understand that often the girls arrive in a grubby state and worse, some have nits, fleas, skin rashes, worms. That is why we require a sample of their stool."

My dad replied: "Then, on arrival, we will help them to clean up in a dignified manner. I will not allow members of staff here to gawk at these young women as if they have arrived to serve a prison sentence. This place is their home for however long they need it. You are their 'house-parent', a parent in lieu of the parents who should be looking after and caring for them but for the circumstance they presently find themselves in -- I hope that I have made myself clear!"

I know that it was not clear to every house-parent; I also noted that those to whom it was not clear, suddenly were gone.

Chapter 29
A Murder
Narrator

Joe. How to describe Joe? He was the type of person who was never noticed. Mild-mannered, no distinguishing features although he was fairly short, nowhere close to two metres in his stocking feet. Dusty, thin, blond hair and a rounded face. He was likeable, but when he was in a room, or a crowd of people, he was not noticeable, and when he was not there his absence was not noticed either! He was shy, of that there was no doubt, he kept himself to himself. No one at The Rose Tree Estate knew anything of his life before he arrived there one snow covered night. The police had found him wandering, in the dark, but no inquiry had found his parents. Joe was too young to explain what circumstance had bought him to a snowy corner on that dark night when a police car with two police constables happened upon him. His nickname at Ash House, the house he had progressed to in the years after his arrival at Willow House, was 'Slow Joe'. It was a lifetime ago, when Nursery Nurse June had greeted the police officer who had handed the cold little fellow over to the care of the council. The nickname was nothing to do with his ability to traverse a terrain; it was his inability to traverse his thoughts from one to another in smooth, or timely, fashion. He would always get to the point, but it took time, the laughter of his fellows gave him great pain and anxiety. He did not often display it, but it was a pressure inside his skull that caused pressure on his brain cells, and sometimes made him mad. Mad to a level of violence, which could lead to the smashing of furniture, and any items that might be in the vicinity when his anger burst out. When it did, he was the polar opposite of the mild, self-effacing, Joe Slow. It was difficult for the house-parents to safely manage such outbursts, many carried scars of these violent episodes, some of Joe's peers would run away, some were excited by the rage and would watch from a distance that they felt was safe.

No one thought that Joe would deliberately hurt anyone, but they recognised the frustration in him, even though some enjoyed winding him up until the spring was released.

He was a very strong young man at this point in the story, he was stocky, he could do push-ups and pull-ups, he was capable of lifting some very heavy weights.

Joe did not mean to do it, it was just that the noise, in his head had become so loud that it had broken out into parts of his brain where it did not belong. He lashed out with his arms and his hands, then it was a poker from beside the fire. He was just so cross with her, she had taunted him, she kept on screaming "Slow Joe, Joe Slow". The snapping inside Joe's skull was like the rattle of a machine gun. His arms punched into her face, one after another, and then she ran out and around to the back of Ash House. The fire-poker was in Joe's hand, and with a downward whipping motion, it was careering into the hair on her head. There was a splatter blood and she fell at his feet. He looked down at her; he looked at the poker in his hand. He realised, after some time had elapsed, that he had done something truly serious. Everything was quiet around him and he thought that was good. He said to himself, 'I had to stop her', then he realised that people were going to be angry about that which he had done.

The girl, was not an adult, she was about the same age as Joe, she was very thin. The reason she taunted Joe was because she thought he was weaker than she was, she thought she could take out her frustrations on him and get away with it. Well, strictly speaking, she did not think this -- she felt it. However, Evelynn had misjudged Joe, he was not the one she should have taken her feelings out on, and now she had paid the highest price and she was dead. There was blood but by chance this incident had occurred at the side of the house where the metal fire escape stood against the building. Further along the wall from it were the dustbins. Joe thought about things for a short while. Then he went to each bin in turn and lifted the lid. When he came to the one next to the 'Pig Swill Bin' he found it was empty. He then made the decision to put Evelynn's body into the bin, hoping that nobody would find out what he had done.

Joe was strong and Evelynn was small and thin, but he struggled to lift Evelynn. He managed to drag her to the bin, then he laid the bin on its side. Bit by bit he pushed her legs and most of her body into the round, galvanised bin. She was too tall to fit completely in. He managed to pull the bin upright, gravity made the lower part of her body slump as her legs collapsed and the corpse settled in position. Then he pushed the bin back against the wall. He tried to push her even further down. Having done all that was possible the upright corpse of Evelynn inside the bin was sitting like Buddha. He lifted the bin lid from the floor and balanced it, as well as he could, on the top of her head, leaning it against the red brick wall which was now behind her. He then made his escape. Of course the bin lid did not balance for very long, it crashed down shortly after Joe Slow's swift departure. The metallic-crashing noise alerted the cook who came out from her kitchen to catch the bizarre sight of Evelynn's corpse protruding from the bin. The cook was mentally traumatised by this gruesome sight.

*

Cook resigned her job and her family felt the chill of lack of income for nearly half a year before she found work elsewhere. She told her friends and relatives that she would never go back to that place. She had seen such violence there. Children fighting and staff who had no idea of how to control them, let alone the youngsters who had absolutely no respect for themselves or anybody else. Finding the dead body of that young girl was the absolute last straw in a catalogue of horrors. She told everyone that she had found boys on The Rose Tree Estate: "Who were not even ten years old sniffing glue, to make themselves high, as if their brains were not damaged enough." She had heard rumours of some of the older children: "Smoking not just tobacco, but marijuana. There was also talk about LSD."

"Where on earth do they get the money from? That's what I would like to know. Here am I with my children to feed, and yet they, the inmates of Rose Tree, have money for drugs!" Complained Heather, former cook name, in her broad West Indian lilt.

"You know what too? I caught two of them teenagers doing sex, doing sex! On the bit of ground up behind Ash House, where that little copse of trees is, they just laughed at me and ran off. Oh no, no, no never again will I look for work in such a place."

*

Evelynn left no one to mourn her. She had no family except the people who lived with her at Ash House.

The police started their investigation, they found blood on Joe's shoes and that was how he was caught. He confessed to what he had done and tried his best to explain the pressure in his head, and how Evelynn had pushed him to his limit until he had to burst. He really did not remember the poker in his hand, or it striking her head.

A 'Lifetime' prison sentence, is a long time, whatever a persons age. For Joe, whose life was really only just starting, the twenty-seven years he would spend in prison passed slowly. He was forty-two years old in two-thousand-and-seven when he was released on parole. There had been drugs available in prison, but he had avoided them whilst inside. Once released, without the safety net of the prison cell, drugs and alcohol stepped up to support him. He was obliged to report to probation once a week, every week for the rest of his life. On occasions, because of the drugs and alcohol, he would miss appointments and there were several times he was returned to prison. He has never murdered since that terrible day in nineteen eighty.

I must warn you against being judgemental, for although Joe had murdered Evelynn, and although Evelynn had taunted Joe until he lashed out, there is a darker part of this story you have yet to be told.

*

It should also be pointed out that the timeline of this story is not linier. The stories of some sometimes overlap, sometimes they did not. There were many houses on the estate and there was not really one 'big-chief' in overall charge. Also remember that The Rose Tree Estate was a living entity itself. Staff came and went, good staff came and went, bad staff came and went. Fashions changed and so did things that worried the population at large. What did not change was that there were always people who needed to be cared for.

Chapter 30
Concussion
Kristopher

Seeing a baby rocking back and forth in a cot is very unsettling, it can even be shocking. Not every baby does it. However, frequently, babies who have been neglected or mistreated often do so. Depending on the cot in which they sleep and the floor upon which the cot stands, the noise can be really disturbing. Due to the advice of the time, the babies were mostly laid tummy-side-down with their nappy clad bottoms set higher than the rest of their bodies. They would rock backwards and forwards, crashing their little heads into the end of the cots. When witnessed for the first time it would be easy to think that the child would cause its brain to be damaged, maybe the brain has already been so damaged by the lack of love they are merely trying to finish the job. It can very, very, distressing to watch.

It is hard to understand how babies, with their super big eyes, and chuckling smiles, could ever invoke the wrath of an adult. You should now that the big eyes and chuckling are part of a baby's defence mechanism.

You might ask, who could harm a child? Who could starve a child? Who could leave a child so dirty that it smells of urine and faeces and it's bottom and genitals are red raw with nappy rash? Who could slap a baby until the bruises are blue and brown? Who could stub out a cigarette on a child's arm? Who could lock a child in a room and leave to go on holiday for a week? Who could leave their baby child in the arms of a perverted man for his sexual gratification in exchange for a couple of twenty pound notes?

You might ask who could do such things? I do not know, I am merely the narrator of this tale. I do know that all these things have happened to children and sadly they keep on happening. So if you have been a fortunate child, or if your childhood was fortunate, lend a thought to those little ones who are not swaddled in love and care. There are children sleeping on the streets in Manila. There are children living in the sewers in Bogotá and Bucharest. There have been children in the Congo enlisted into the army who are given guns and bullets and who are taught to shoot and kill.

When you come to sensational news stories, which reflect upon the worst of inhumanity. Understand that behind the headlines are real people, and many of them have been hurt and damaged far beyond the experiences of most people. When you read of Joe Slow, Grace, Evelynn, Isoken, Adam and others you have yet to meet on these pages, spare a thought, give them, at least, a little more latitude, understand that the circumstances which they have survived may have been harsher then those of your own experience. Yes it is true that we all have to play the hand we are dealt, but empathy is a virtue, if you have to feel good about you to have any chance of being empathetic; if you can please be so. Some do make it through like Reynesh they find purpose and build on the poor start they had. Not every one is as strong as Reynash. Remember too that not every hour of every life is coated in disaster.

Chapter 31
Session Twelve: To the Isle of Wight
Kristopher

"I know it was a children's home, well an estate of children's homes. I know that many of the people, staff and children alike, were those who did not have the luxury of a functioning family, mum, dad and siblings. I know some came from the poorest of backgrounds, and some had been abused, physically and mentally before they arrived at The Rose Tree Estate, but, although they came with difficulties, there was much to help each person. The environment was actually one of safety in comparison to some places the occupants had been in before. I know not all the house-parents, and other staff, were as good as they should have been, some were cruel and some evil, but I think that it should be made clear that The Rose Tree Estate had many good points, and that many were very much better off by being there than they would otherwise have been elsewhere.

The grounds were beautiful and the facilities were superb. The physical environment was palace-like in contrast to the places some residents had come from."

"The world had different taboos and mores back then. In terms of how long it takes people to get used to new groups of people. The *Windrush* had only just docked with its cargo of Caribbean men and women who had come to help rebuild Britain after the Second World War. That war was only a decade in the past when I gained my first memories of Nut Tree House. The first of Britain's 'Race Relations Acts' was not close to being passed back then, that would not come along until nineteen-sixty-five."

"All about me, when I was so young, was a multi-ethnic, multi-cultural society. It was normal to me. I knew nothing of colour-bars. I did not *see 'No Dogs', 'No Irish', 'No coloureds'* in windows in places around where I lived. I did see such signs when dad took me on one of his jobs to see the relatives of once girl, I think her name was Monica, as I told you before, I would wait, for what seemed like hours, in the car. I had asked my dad what the writing said. He told me, he read the board in the window of a house. I asked: 'Does that mean there are no dogs, no Irish and no coloureds in the building? What are Irish? What are coloureds?' He said: "The Irish are people that come from a place called

Ireland. Coloureds is a word used, sometimes unkindly, to describe people who have darker skin than we do. The sign is there to tell people who are looking to rent a room that dogs, Irish and Coloureds should not apply."

"That has always burned in a corner of my brain. For the girls at Nut Tree House, who had darker skin than me, were all very nice to me. I wondered why anybody would not want to rent them a room."

*

"My mum took a group of the girls on a holiday. I went too. We got on the train, it was a wet day, it was a steam train and it took us all the way to Portsmouth. When we passed out into the countryside I remember my mum telling me that the cows were lying down, she said that was a sure sign that it would rain."

"We then got onto the ferry and sailed off to the Isle of Wight. You cannot possibly know what an adventure this was for us all. None of us had done anything like this before; trains, countryside, ferries across the sea and a trip to an island. It was as big a deal as going to the moon as far as we were concerned.

"The journey took the best part of the day. It was coming on the evening when we arrived at the bed and breakfast, a big Victorian house on a quiet street in Ventnor. Mum pulled the doorbell handle and a loud bell jangled. To the door was answered by a man, smartly dressed in a white jacket and bow tie, who had a cigarette hanging from his bottom lip. Mum introduced herself and then the girls and me. The last person she introduced was Rosetta, a girl of about seventeen years, whose parents had been killed in a road accident. They had come to Britain from Jamaica and Rosetta had skin that was very much darker than mine. My mum told the man Rosetta's name, in response the man said: 'Well that is all well and good but she can't stay here, the others, you and your son are welcome, but I won't have 'coloureds' in here, this is a respectable house. You should have made it clear when you made the booking'."

Doctor Samuels said: "Hard to believe that that was allowed then, it is not that long ago, and you witnessed this ugly moment. How did it affect you?"

I replied: "Well I am not sure really, it is only with hindsight, and speaking to you about this, that I can being to grapple with such an awful idea. Rosetta was really good with me; she played with me and read to me, I liked her. Mum had to go off knocking on doors of other bed and breakfasts until she found one which would let Rosetta stay. It took a long time. So the other house-parent, who had come on the trip with us, had to go with Rosetta and stay in a different place from the rest of us. Apart from that it was really wonderful time. It was warm and sunny, we went to the beech and went into the sea. We went to *Alum Bay* and filled little glass tubes with the different coloured sands. We went on a boat ride to *Black Gang Chime* and the man who drove the boat told us all about smugglers and pirates.

There was none of the health and safety of today, we just climbed in the open boat, no life jackets, and off we went out onto the sea, speeding fast through the water. The captain sat with a cigarette hanging out of his mouth as he held the tiller.

We ate breakfast; bacon, sausage, eggs, beans, toast and milk. Lunchtime I do not remember, oh! of course it was bed and breakfast not lunch, 'half pension' I think that was. In the evening we would have our evening meal at the bed and breakfast, I think they called that 'full pension'. Most of it was fine but then they bought oxtail soup to us and I did not like it. Strange how I remember that, I have never liked oxtail soup to this day.

They used to sell that oxtail soup in tins, Oxen were cows, bulls which had been castrated and they were used to pull ploughs or carts. I do not know how many oxen were ploughing fields when I was a boy; it was surely tractors by then.

The man who told Rosetta she could not stay never stopped smoking, he had a machine, a small silver box, to make the cigarettes. In the box was tobacco and papers he would lick along a sticky edge of the paper then put the paper into a roller in the box lid, he would then put tobacco on the paper and then shut the box -- a cigarette would then appear on the roller through the top of the box. He let me do this for him once I had to learned how to do it, so by the time we left, he had a good number of 'roll-ups' as he called them. I was fascinated by the great knots of skin he had on his face, like a balloon if you pinch a small piece through two fingers. These knots were darker than the skin on the rest of his oval bald head. He also had the shakes; he would shudder and tremble every once in a while. Mum told me he had an illness called *Parkinson's*.

Chapter 32
Arthur and Benjamin.
Narrator

"How could anyone understand Arthur?" Asked Benjamin. "The filth and the smell, the cockroaches, the rats. Dad going off, then mum dying."

Arthur spoke.

"You always looked out for me Benjamin, thank goodness you are my brother. I thought I had gone to heaven when we arrived on Rose Tree. It was like we'd become millionaires. You know one of the things that really shocked me that first night? Sheets. I had never seen sheets. They were all crisp; matron said that was because of the starch. I had never heard that word before."

Benjamin chipped in: "Matron Monica. She was lovely. I'd never met anyone that kind before. I could not get to sleep that first night. Everything was so strange, although the main thing, Arthur, was; I had never slept in a bed on my own. Sheets and blankets.

Mum used to throw coats over us, do you remember? Then there was food. The first time we had seen cornflakes, you didn't know to put milk and sugar on them, and the other kids laughed."

"They were laughing at you too Benjamin, lets be honest you had never seen breakfast cereal before either. Do you remember that sluice room where they took our old clothes away and hosed us down when we arrived? They cut all our hair off to get rid of the lice. It seems so long ago but it could have been yesterday. What year did we go there Benjamin?"

"Well let's work it out. You are eighty-five now and I am eighty-six. You were four years old when we went there and I was five. It is two-thousand and sixteen now so it was nineteen thirty-five and we stayed there for twelve years, Arthur, all the way through the war."

"I would say they were twelve good years Benjamin. We had a roof, food, warmth and a good time with the other kids. The house-parents cared for us and set us on a good road." Arthur reminisced fondly.

"We went straight from there into business. Rose Tree even gave us our first paid job. Remember? We decorated the gatekeeper's cottage." Said Benjamin.

"Before long." responded Arthur. "We were doing jobs all over the area. *Arthur and Benjamin Cardoso for all your decorating needs."*

Benjamin poured them both another glass of single malt whisky; they sat in their leather armchairs, by the fire, in their very nice home. The walls were lined with bookcases and the curtains were red velvet. They had always been together, they never married, brothers who started life in the most meagre of ways, but finished their days in riches which they had earned all by themselves.

Chapter 33
Who has Been Sleeping in my Bed?
Narrator

Sister Magdalene had only just arrived at The Rose Tree Estate. She had little idea of what to expect. She had joined the convent when she had been twenty-three years old. She had been to a good private school and had then learned short hand and typing which enabled her to get a job as a secretary in an estate agents business. It was not what she wanted. She wanted to give her life to God. She found a religious order and they accepted her into her period of testing, known as *Postulancy*. It was established that she did, indeed, have a vocation to the life of a nun, and so she began to wear her black and white habit and she undertook the *novitiate*. After two years she took her *temporary vows*. After four years she petitioned to make her *Perpetual Profession* and so she took her *Solemn Vows* when she was then thirty-one years old.

Her experience of life was limited, but she had had a good education and she had a loving family. She had had no relationship of any sexual kind. She really knew nothing of such things. When she arrived at the front door of Birch House, on The Rose Tree Estate. One boy called out:

"None of this, none of that...", whilst another boy completed the sentence with, "....and none of the other!"

Sister Magdalene had no idea what the boys were sniggering at.

The next morning it was Sister Magdalene's job to wake all the young women and start to get them ready for the day, making sure all were washed, dressed and tidy berfore breakfast.

Birch House had a lot of small bedrooms, each for two people and fitted with bunk beds. Each bedroom looked out over the big garden.

The sister knocked on the first door and opened it. To her surprise, and to her horror, the top bunk held two bodies. A girl who should have been there, and a boy, who should not! The boy was awake in an instant and he lept onto the windowsill, out of the window and down the drainpipe. The girl sat up in bed and wondered if she should say anything.

Sister Magdalene was unsure of what she should do in this situation. It was her first real day, she had been on duty overnight, but she had slept and nothing had disturbed her, certainly not a boy climbing in through a window to sleep in the same bed as one of the girls. Was that her fault she asked herself? Maybe he was a relative, or some boy who had no home to go to. She wished that the Reverend Mother had been on hand to advise her. She had only been here a few hours and already two boys, she guessed, had been making fun of her, and now this. She was very sure that the incident was not a good thing but then how would it be if she got this girl into trouble, or would it be that boy who got her in to trouble? That is what they had told her boys do. What did they mean by that?

"Sister," said the girl, "I am sorry, that boy is my younger brother. He was scared so he slept with me. He had nowhere to sleep last night. Please don't tell, they might think you have not been doing your job very well!"

Monica could spin a line and tell a lie without pausing for breath and this was a lie. Sister Magdalene swallowed it with the hook, line and sinker. Indeed she was most grateful.

Monica and her boyfriend got away with it but Sister Magdalene did confess to the local priest that she thought she was guilty of naïvety. She said to the priest that another boy had told her a joke but she did not understand.

"There were three nuns, a man jump out and exposed himself to them. One fainted, one had a heart attack and the other had a stroke! Can you explain that to me father?"

The priest told her to say three Hail Mary's and to think on it no more.

It was a tough environment for a woman dressed in black and white. She was not one of the robust types of nun who were able to command and get others to do God's bidding. No, she was the 'deferring' sort who always wanted to do good, the one who was naïve, and that all the young people could take advantage of.

Then a riot occurred. There was a particularly fractious group of girls who were unhappy with themselves, with everybody and with everything else. Sister Magdalene was about to lock the kitchen door and go up to her bed when the three girls appeared from nowhere. Sister Magdalene found herself being pushed into the door, the door swung in and so did the four of them.

"What is all this about?" Demanded the nun from within her wimple.

"We want the key to the fridge, we are hungry and thirsty." Stated one of the girls.

"Well you know that the fridge and he kitchen are locked each night, you had your supper Jane, you three should be in bed. Now off you go." ordered the Sister.

Sonja spoke. "No, give me the key to the fucking fridge or."

"Or what?" Asked the sister.

"I'll stick you with this." Screeched Jane as she pulled a sheath knife from its leather holster which was on her belt, but to the back, so Sister Magdalene had not noticed it.

"Now you put that down Sonja. That is not the way to do things. What are you thinking? You cannot threaten people with a knife. Put it back in the sheath."

"After you have given us the key to the fridge." Said another of the quartet.

"It's OK." said Pauline, as the last, Yvonne, lunged forward and grabbed the keys from the nun's hand.

The sister was powerless, she prayed for a miracle but none arrived instantly. Pauline unlocked the fridge and the three helped themselves to a pint of milk each, and they cut into an apple pie with Sonja's sheath knife.

It was just then that God's miracle did arrive in the shape of Mrs. Matherson, who was now standing and filling up the doorway like a giant gene from the lamp. Mrs. Matherson had been in the Wrens during the war. She had the air of authority which was denied to Sister Magdalene, a huge voice and a terrifying countenance. She was a large women, physically, and a large woman emotionally. She had a presence that was felt by all in a room before she even entered it. Whenever she arrived it was like a front door being blown in by an ice-cold gale from the north.

"What on earth is going on here, may I ask?" She boomed.

If Sister Magdalene had said such a phrase all three girls would have answered back, in unison. "What does it look like?" Now they were dealing with Matherson, the courage and boldness of the four girls vaporised and floated away to heaven looking for forgiveness.

"I will see you four outside my office at O-seven-hundred-hours in the morning, wear your school PT kit. You will be going on a run. Be late and woe-betide you. Now to bed, I will be visiting your rooms in ten minutes. Brush your teeth; wash your face, and lights out immediately. *MOVE*"

The girls vanished as their boldness had vaporised.

Mrs. Matherson now turned her attention to the Nun.

"Your bother Sister Magdalene is that you do not realise that your softly, softly, gentle approach is not what these young women need, or want. They are here in Birch House, on The Rose Tree Estate because they have pushed the boundaries of society, their parents, their schools and the police so hard they have been sent here, no one can cope with them. They need a firm hand, some rules, some discipline. Giving them *lar di da* choices, *'would you like it like this or that'. NO sister* -- you tell them the way that it is going to be, never change once you have set the boundary. These kids will be alright, eventually, but we just have to give them a few walls that will not crumble, unlike their crumbly parents, and their crumbly teachers, and the crumbly police force. They all tried and they all failed these young women. You are working here with me now sister, buck-up and get a backbone. We have a duty not to fail those for whom we care. You do these children no favours by giving into them. They are scared because they have been given no firm boundaries.

Young people need strong guiding hands, that is really love, not your namby-pamby nonsense that God will still love you even if you beat up your grandmother. They curse me, and they will get cold tomorrow, we can expect snow according to the *'Home Service'* weather forecast. So those girls will get cold and they will curse me all the more, but a few years from now they will remember this incident. If they remember you at all it will be with a great snigger of laughter, and a few words around the 'pathetic edge' of the spectrum. On the other hand, they will remember me as the only one who really understood them, and the one who was strong enough to stop them."

The Sister listened in silence. She knew that what Mrs. Matherson said was true in every detail. She was was unsure how to gain the surety that Matherson possessed, how does one build such an inner self-confidence? She asked herself.

Matherson continued: "I know these girls Sister Magdalene, I was one of them once. No one could control me and I ended up here, in Birch House on The Rose Tree Estate. The War sorted me out. Being in the Wrens. Sister, most people are not that complicated, they need food, clothes, and somewhere to keep out of the cold and wet. What they need more than those things is to be loved and valued; constantly being nice to someone is not necessarily loving them, Sister. Loving them is being strong and pulling them up sharp when they are being naughty. Never once do you need to use physical violence, never once do you need to touch these girls. When they are good always offer praise and remember, and remind them that you have not forgotten on occasion. When they are bad, give swift punishment that challenges them physically and emotionally. Then leave it and never bring it up again."

The Sister said: "Well I wish I could, but Pauline had a knife!"

"Yes I know, she whittles, have you not seen all the things she makes? Some of the items are exquisite. Mushrooms or a wooden doll from a bit of Silver Birch. I think she could whittle just about any shape or form. She sells them at The Rose Tree Estate Christmas Market. That will be next week, make sure you buy one. Good night Sister.

Chapter 34
From the Brothel.
Narrator

Bridget was a teenager, fourteen years old, when she arrived on The Rose Tree Estate in nineteen eighty-two. She had been arrested by police who had raided a brothel one weekend. Bridget claimed she was there to help make the tea, but it turned out that she was providing sexual favours, for money and that she had been having sex with men for over a year in that place.

Bridget was slim and blonde; she had an attractive face, which would have been worthy of the cinema screen. Her mother had been a prostitute, she did not know who her father was. She had learned to care for herself and knew much about survival.

Nobody on The Rose Tree Estate would dare to mess with her, she did not have to do anything to create such respect, people just looked at her -- and they knew.

She knew what men were like, and she kept a detailed account of the people who had been her clients and what their secret desires were. It was her insurance policy. If she ever had a client who was unwilling to provide a tip, she would remind them of her age and her ability to inform the police, anonymously, of their proclivity and, she added if any thing 'fatal' should over come her a copy of her notes was ready to be delivered to the authorities.

Here on The Rose Tree Estate Bridget saw that there could be a business opportunity. She realised that there was a way to make money out of sex without having to have sex. All she had to do was to get a house-parent into a situation where she and they were alone together and then threaten to blackmail them for things that they had not done. She did this with one man and one woman who were house-parents. Bridget was careful not to overdo things, she took five pounds a month from each of them, average earnings then were about six thousand pounds a year.

Bridget also arranged a similar thing with a teacher at her school, and once in a while she would turn a trick, and put the money into her post office book.

Chapter 35
Marie.
Narrator

Marie spent the whole of her childhood on The Rose Tree Estate. She did not know who her parents were. In nineteen fifty-eighty she was placed in care. Things went fairly well, she went to school and then she got a job and a place to live, it was not too bad.

She enjoyed working the tills at the supermarket in Streatham, South London. It was a famous store; the owner claimed that it was the first Supermarket in Britain. Her colleagues were friendly and she settled in quickly and it was not long before she found a boyfriend.

She liked him because she found him dangerous, she was not sure at first why he was dangerous, but after a few months she started to understand.

It was always an early start to get up and go to work. The young men and women who made up the staff of the supermarket needed to be on the premises well before the doors opened to customers. There was dusting and cleaning to do in addition to making sure all the shelves were properly stacked. It was a long day for all of them.

Then, one morning, just as Marie was about to leave for work, there was a banging on her door. She opened it and there was Gary, her boyfriend. He seemed to be out of breath and his face was bruised. There was a cut above his eye and it was red with blood. He held out his hand to Marie. He was holding a black bag. He said:

"Marie, I need you to take care of this, hide it somewhere, no need to look inside, I will be back."

With that, Gary was gone. Marie had no idea what to make of this, but she loved him, so she made a space at the back of her wardrobe into which she put the bag and went to work.

After a week she began to worry about Gary, she did not usually worry because he often worked away -- well that is what he led her to believe. Marie had no telephone and she seldom got letters, she was not sure if Gary could write, even if he wanted to. She did not know where he lived.

A month went by. One day, just finished eating her evening meal, there was a banging on her front door. She thought; 'at last' and went to open it. A posse of uniformed policemen pushed past her and a man in ordinary clothes showed her a police warrant card, Marie had never seen such a thing before, he also had a sheet of paper which, he said was a warrant to search her property. Marie was bewildered and extremely scared. She stood unable to move her legs.

After an eternity, or so it seemed, the policeman in plain clothes, spoke to her. He said:

"Marie Smith, I am arresting you for the possession of a firearm and stolen money to the value of three thousand pounds."

He did say other things but Marie had no idea what words came from his mouth she was in total and utter shock.

At the police station she met a solicitor and she told him what had happened. She told him that Gary had asked her to take care of the bag and that he told her not to look in it. She told him that the last time she had seen Gary was a month before when he gave her the bag. She told him that she had nothing to do with it, she was just minding it for her boyfriend.

The police would give her no information as to how they had come to her, or if they knew where Gary was. She could not tell them where he lived and the description she gave would have been a good fit for many other young men who hovered about south London at that time.

The case was serious, a loaded weapon and such a large sum of money in the possession of a girl of Jamaican heritage. She was threatened with the Crown Court. The police were blatant in their pressure, saying that if she agreed to make a guilty plea in court then they would forget the charges of soliciting.

Marie said: "What soliciting? What do you mean?"

The policemen in the ordinary clothes looked Marie up and down and said:

"Come on Marie, we know you come from The Rose Tree Estate, we know that you are a prostitute, and not only that, you have been caught with a loaded gun and a pile of cash. You do not even know the surname of this Gary you keep talking about. We had an anonymous call from one of your punters. So your best chance is to come clean. Tell the judge you did it and he will let you off with a lighter sentence."

Marie could not have felt more alone, she was frightened, she was more scared than she had ever been. She could not bear the cell in which she had been caged. So when the Clerk of the Court asked her to plead she said "guilty". The judge, in his wig and red cape, looked down his nose at this small little black girl and said some scathing things about her. He then sentenced her to a long term in prison.

The injustice served its time with Marie. When released life for her was so difficult. Getting a job with a criminal record seemed impossible. She did not understand why finishing the prison sentence was not the end of the matter. She objected to the cruelty that every sentence is a life sentence. She never saw Gary again, she never had a boyfriend again. and in twenty thousand and fifteen, she received a letter from the Department of Work and Pensions advising her that the United Kingdom had shifted the goal posts, yet again, and raised the retirement age for women to sixty five years.

Marie started life with a bad set of cards. A month after she received that letter, the police broke down the door to her bedsit and found her decaying body slumped in a chair, the letter had fallen onto the floor beside her.

Chapter 36
Archibald
Narrator

Archibald Anderson picked up the newspaper and his post from his doormat and went back into the kitchen he shared with himself. He glanced at the headline for the eighteenth of July nineteen seventy-five. An American and a Russian spacecraft had docked together in space in a first for the two nations who were normally at loggerheads. It was his birthday, but the letters contained no cards or greetings marking the event. Today he was fifty-five years old. He had been just of age to join the army and fight in the Second World War. He rose in the ranks and became a sergeant.

In mid November nineteen forty-one Archibald was at the siege of Tobruk, fighting against the forces of Rommel.

None of his fellow soldiers knew that he was a homosexual, none knew of his fantasies concerning young boys.

As an army sergeant he was a strict disciplinarian. He stood no nonsense from anyone. His soldiers loved him and hated him in equal measure. Empathy was nothing to Archibald, to him he had had a tough life and it was doing nobody any favours to allow them an easy time.

Archibald poured another cup of coffee and opened his letters. The first was from The London Borough

Council confirming his appointment as Warden of Hornbeam House on The Rose Tree Estate. His appointment was to begin on Monday 4th of August. (Remember Amelia and Gary from Chapter nineteen. Gary was a young man living in Hornbeam House in the care of Archibald when Amelia became pregnant.)

Hornbeam was a House where difficult young men and boys were put. Archibald vowed at his interview to bring discipline to the chaos and anarchy that he had witnessed during his visit to the home.

That is exactly what he did. To say that he put The Fear of God into those boys would be an understatement. Six months into the job and the Powers, at Childcare Services, hailed Archibald's conquest of Hornbeam House as their greatest success.

Archibald ruled Hornbeam House as a dictator. Punishment for the smallest of felonies was swift and severe. Boys would be excluded from the activities they most enjoyed. They would be locked in the cellar in solitary confinement. They were denied food and made to do strenuous physical exercise. Then there was the slipper or the cane across a naked backside. Archibald kept no records of these punishments and he kept the boys so frightened, none would dare tell tales out of school. He suffered no nonsense from his staff either. They toed his line or they found another place to work. Hornbeam House was spick and span, 'clean as a bum fresh from a French bidet', was how Archibald called it. Some of the boys learned of the harshest punishment of all. None told of their experience for fear that it would be repeated. Everyone knew that if they heard Archibald's steps in the corridor, outside the dormitory after lights-out, they had to cross their fingers and hope it was not their name that he called.

Everyone knew that if Archibald came in the night it meant a trip to his store cupboard for one of them. No one ever reported what happened to them in that room for Archibald filled their minds with all manner of horrors should they betray the secret. Once the sexual activity had ceased, and Archibald was satisfied that the boy was sufficiently scared, he would give the boy a bar of chocolate, with five boy faces on the wrapper, and send him back to bed. Five Boy's chocolate bars had five pictures of a boy on the wrapper showing five expressions, Desperation – Pacification – Expectation – Acclamation – Relaization, many people would find the pictures disturbing.

The boy's of Hornbeam House had their own uniform, they were forbidden to mix with the children of the other houses on The Rose Tree Estate. They had a reputation around the Rose Tree, and in the village, as the most polite of the children from Rose Tree.

The pressure under which the Hornbeam House boys lived was immense. There were not many people in Childcare Services who could have pulled-off this feat. He knew, and his employers knew, that if Archibald were not in charge of Hornbeam House, the social structure there would collapse and that would have a terrible effect upon all the other homes on the estate. Archibald had created a position for himself which was as secure as a position could be. There was nobody capable of filling his shoes. Nobody dare challenge his authority; nobody took any heed of gossip or rumour regarding the corporal punishment or the infamous store cupboard. Even when one boy threw himself from an upstairs window, in an attempt to commit suicide, did anyone question Archibald's methods, motivation, or results. Of course in nineteen seventy-five no one could see what kind of adults the boys of Hornbeam House would turn out to be.

*

A Letter to Mr Archibald Anderson.
Narrator

Dear Mr Archibald Anderson,

Sir. Along with all the other boys of Hornbeam House, typing classes were mandatory for me. So now that I have left Hornbeam House, and The Rose Tree Estate, I am writing this to you on a typewriter so that you will not be able to recognise my handwriting.

I want to let you know just how much I hated my time at Hornbeam House. I would say that there is nothing wrong with Hornbeam House, expect for you and the members of your Gestapo staff.

Many of the young boys who came to you had suffered great calamity before they reached your door. In my own case I became an orphan because my parents had died. I responded in a way that was considered disruptive and so I was pushed into Hornbeam House. I wanted the love my parents had given me, what I got was a living hell.

Mr. Anderson, you are a bully and you are evil. Even though I left Hornbeam House a while ago, I am terrified, for I know that if you ever found out where, and who I am, you would hunt me down.

I have written to the authorities, even though I am so scared.

That is what the time I spent with you did to us, and many of my fellows, it made us even more scared than we were when first arrived

For what you did to me in your store cupboard I would dearly love to kill you. Expect a visit from the police Mr. Anderson because they are coming to get you.

Chapter 37
The Enquiry Starts.
Narrator

The Independent Enquiry was instigated by the Home Secretary. It was 2013 and Mrs. Claudia Kemsing had been in office for three years. It had been a twenty-seven-year-long road from being a councillor in a south London borough, to one of the high offices of state. Kemsing was a hard right-winger, Conservative, with all the baggage that comes with that. Her husband was a businessman of millionaire proportions.

In her heart of hearts she was a Church of England member, first of all, who thought everyone was middle class, she had been to Oxford University, where she met her husband, Gregory. She was the scholarship girl, whom was looked down upon by many of her well heeled university colleagues. The thing was that she had never been very comfortable within herself. She was interested in clothes and jewellery and had a constant requirement to have new, fashionable, couture about her. Even when she had been a councillor, nearly three decades before, she never really understood that the way she dressed put up a barrier between her and those constituents who were getting by on benefits. The truth is she never really understood why anyone was poor. She was a soul who could empathise with nobody. The other big thing in her mind was that

England was primarily for the English. She made exceptions in her mind for those foreigners who came from abroad to work, after all, there were definitely jobs which English people should not been allowed to do. As for the heathen Scots, the barmy Welsh and the uncontainable Northern Irish, and heavens, the *Irish-Irish*, none of them could ever be a patch on the great Englishmen who had conquered the far reaches of the planet and made The Empire.

As far as Claudia was concerned, foreigners who were needed should be allowed to stay whilst any who were not should be sent back from whence they came.

Of course she would never say any of this out loud, she was not stupid, she knew what to say, and when, and to whom to say it. That is why she was now the Home Secretary -- that and the fact that she was fully aware of an affair the Prime Minister had had with an intern four years before her appointment, her silence being exchanged for this rather well paid position. She relished the power and the prospect of great dividends once she had vacated politics and returned to the real world of business. At the moment, though, she had her hands on the levers that could make prospective immigrants lives very difficult. She was so proud of the task force she had instigated the Home Office Removal Service. Who would, in the dead of night, remove sleeping aliens from their beds and whisk them off on to a plane before they could say refugee.

She would never admit it in the House of Commons, but all her staff, including thousands of enforcement officers she had had employed, knew exactly what the Home Secretary had in mind and most of them were happy to earn their livings by carrying out her bidding.

The Home Secretary was a real mixture of personality types;

by contrast to the fashion icon, that she thought she was; a never ending wardrobe of expensive couture, bright colours and sparkling jewellery, the fun loving personality, it was widely reported that Claudia Kemsing was meticulous in her devotion to her duty and to exploring every corner of her red box each night, with her cup of coco, before she went off to bed. That takes some serious orderliness in personality traits. It is seldom, if at all, that these two facets display in dominate form in the same person, unless that person is really troubled in mind. Looking deeper into her personality other parts were also at juxtaposition positions. On the one hand she found it extremely difficult to make a decision, and even more difficult to keep to that decision, yet almost at the same time, she could make instant decisions and never dream of changing them. She became renowned for saying one thing one day, only to say the exact opposite a few days later; maybe this was the result of years of training as a politician -- trying to be all things to all people.

The crucial thing anyone had to know about the Home Secretary was that she was totally in charge, of every fine detail. Delegate, she had no clue as to what that meant.

Gregory, her husband, and Claudia lived a life which was far beyond the expectations of ninety-five percent of the world's population and, as long as they were able, their plan was to keep on enjoying it. Gregory knew his place, his wife was the boss and if he just did as she bade, there was nothing wrong in his life.

For a politician, Claudia knew absolutely nothing about so called 'ordinary people', but actually that is not uncommon amongst the political class.

It was not long after she had taken up her position as Home Secretary that her personal private secretary produced a pile of files relating to sexual impropriety by previous members of both the House of Lords and the House of Commons, there were some current members named as well. Mrs. Kemsing made copious notes about who did what to whom, what, where, why and how. After her studies were complete she told her personal private secretary to personally destroy all the evidence, (she had not meant to say *evidence*, that just slipped out,) she had meant to tell him to burn the lot, and tell no one what he had done. Claudia was ambitious and she knew that all these awful secrets could prove useful, she was now a party too, would come handy, she also knew she did not need the documents, for just knowing what was written on the document would be enough to frighten the perpetrators into any corner she chose. With all the documents destroyed, they could never be linked back to her. She knew that some of what she now knew would be very useful as she climbed up, and over, all the other candidates to become Prime Minister, wouldn't that make her daddy proud? In her heart she knew it probably would not, for nothing about her had ever pleased him. She even over heard him saying to one of his golfing pals that a son always makes a better child and that Claudia was not a girl with the fairest facial features. That criticism was the shifting sands of foundation upon which her life had been built, ninety-nine point nine recurring think that their daughter is the most precious, beautiful, creature they have ever been near. Not Claudia's dad. Those words cut into her and screwed up her personality, they turned her inside out. Never comfortable in her own skin, never truly being herself, always maintaining an act. An act to hide the real Claudia from the world. She would ensure that the abrasive sharp exterior would never allow anyone too become to close, and never would she project what she intended to do next.

*

"Who are all these people?" Asked Claudia of her private secretary.

"Well Home Secretary they are a very vocal group who have found their way into the red-top newspapers, which you would, obviously, not have seen, Marm. They claim to be terribly distressed by things which happened to them whilst they were in the care of the London County Council."

Claudia gave a puzzled squint and then said:

"The London County Council, that was around when I was still in primary school. Then they changed it to the Greater London Council; Maggie hated Ken Livingstone so she bulldozed that to oblivion. So who took over from them?"

"Well a mixture of Local Authorities, on one of whom you served as a councillor before you were elevated to Westminster, Home Secretary."

"So what has all this to do with me? Surely it is local authority stuff, they should complain to their local authorities."

"They have already, Home Secretary, they have given up on them, but as you were the local councillor when some of these people say they were abused, they are knocking at your door. I really do think you should engage with this ma'am, I think it may well have serious consequences for you."

Claudia started to read the folder of papers. Her private secretary stood at ease by the Home Secretary's great oak desk. The whole room was a leftover from the days of empire, it had a comforting smell, and a grandeur set to intimidate any unfortunate who had requested an audience with the high-end of government. Wooden panels and high bookshelves lining the walls loaded with a huge array of large leather-bound books.

After fifteen minutes the Home Secretary looked up and she said:

"My God, are you sure you burnt all that stuff I gave you, it was the third week I was here? Everything was destroyed? Nothing kept back?"

"Everything was destroyed Home Secretary." Replied the private secretary, whose name was Philip Kenton.

"Thank heavens for that." Claudia continued reading. Then she asked.

"Why did I not hear about this before? This must have been cooking for a long while. What is it they want?"

"They want an Independent public enquiry."

"Do they have any idea what that would cost? This is mostly down to that blaggard whom Maggie was so fond of. The weird, disc jockey, the one who dyed his hair and smoked cigars. Awful man, I met him once. Well I am going to discuss this with the prime minister before I make any decisions. I think you need to make me an appointment, very soon, the council elections are coming up and this story will not do us any good at all.

Heavens! It went on for years, although from what I have glanced at, the seventies and eighties seem to be the worst of it. Well it is quiet shocking! A good twenty years, and how many people were affected? How could anyone do those things to a child in their care? For that matter, how could any adult abuse a child? Philip, I know what many people think of me, I really do not care, but I would care if they were to ever say I failed in my duty towards these people. I know they think I am a bitch, but this is something that needs putting right in some way. The question is how can you put this right? I know what the PM will say. Give them some money, that's his cure for everything. I think I should talk with the chancellor too."

*

The date of the enquiry was set. However, it was very difficult to find people who were willing to get involved and people to run it. Many did not like the idea of having their names associated with child abuse. They did not wish that every time their name was mentioned, the tale would be 'you know her, she was a part of the Child Sexual Abuse Enquiry.' Leaving people to wonder *what part* of the enquiry? Finding someone to head-up the enquiry was also very difficult. Finding someone who was neutral, who had sufficient experience and legal knowledge, and who just happened to have the next five years, or so, free in their dairy. Someone who would be strong enough to listen to many harrowing tales that no one should ever have to hear. Three women were asked, one after the other. Each, in turn, said yes but each threw in the towel before the enquiry started. So Claudia was pleased to find the forth candidate. Who said that she would start the enquiry and run it until all the evidence had been heard, and conclusions drawn. She would then report her findings. However, the compensation package had to be a very substantial she told Claudia.

*

In a way enquiries are much the same and yet all very different from one another. This enquiry was to be open to the general public; it was agreed that any person who had a grievance would have the opportunity to be heard if they wished. It was also agreed that anyone taking part could be represented by a lawyer.

The justification for a public enquiry is the existence of "public concern" about an event or series of events. In this case it was a very large number of events which had taken place over many decades, but principally during the nineteen-seventies and eighties. During the course of the enquiry it emerged that there were a few cases from the previous decade as well. Much of it was to do with The Rose Tree Estate, although that was not an exclusive venue, nor was the timeframe exact either way. So it was decided that it would be an *Independent Public Enquiry.*

*

In all it took five years to get the *Independent Public Enquiry* organised. The venue chosen for the public hearings was a large and ornate, conference room in a building between the Houses of Parliament and Victoria in Westminster. A room full of dark polished wood panelling and rows of sturdy wooden chairs for members of the public and those who wanted to speak. At the top was a large walnut table set on a raised dais so that it sat higher than the rest of the room and which gave the chairperson an air of authority. There was a smaller, separate, table and chair from which witnesses could tell their stories, to the left of the chairperson's table. To the right was a similar set up for the person who was recording all that was said. Sound and video recordings were to be made.

Despite looking somewhat like a courtroom the atmosphere was formal but not unfriendly. The room was generally intimidating, but it had also a warm glow from the walnut coloured wooden furniture.

The public hearings were just one aspect of the enquiry. There were investigations in to various allegations, testimony was collected from people who did not want to come the hearings, or who were unable to get to them. Hearsay evidence was also collected from surviving relatives and friends of people who were deceased. A website was started and stories of victims were collected and edited, some identifying details were changed. Some people felt that their stories had been simplified and that detail had been left out, but those who worked on these stories felt that some of what they had redacted would do more harm than good if displayed for all the world to read on the World Wide Web.

It was far from easy for those charged with doing the work of collecting the stories and sanitising them enough for a general audience. Indeed, the group members found that they became a very close-knit team and they supported each other. There were moments when the tears could not be held back, and there were times in the night when sleep was stolen by the memories of the stories read that day, of inhumanity towards tiny children who needed love and kindness, but who received nothing but unkindness and evil.

One of the main things victims wanted was to be heard and another was to be believed. For many had tried to tell their stories before but they could find no one to listen.

Thousands of documents and hundreds of stories were collected and catalogued.

Then came a huge announcement from a local London authority which had inherited responsibility from the now defunct previous authority. They agreed to pay compensation to all victims, regardless, of severity, and without time limit as to when the abuse happened. They would pay ten thousand pounds per person. Some felt this was generous, and there were those who thought the amount was an insult and not enough for what they had been subjected to. Some claimed that the treatment they had been subjected to was more severe than the treatment experienced by some of their other house-mates and that they should, therefore, receive more money by way of compensation.

*

On the morning of the first public hearing, the television cameras were waiting on the steps of the enquiry building. The journalists were all ready, looking for stories to shock and to sell to their newspapers, television, and radio programmes. People had made the effort dressing in Sunday best. When all the seats had been filled and the usher had closed the doors the first person to be called to speak surprised everybody with what she had to say. No one could see her face because she was hidden behind a screen. Her name was not revealed either.

Patricia had not used that name since nineteen seventy-five. She changed it about then and began what she had hoped would be a new life. It had been OK, she thought, but compared to what? What she felt deeply in her heart was that if only they had not been caught, if only the police had not been involved, she and Dara could have had a great life together. Why, she had asked herself every day for the last forty-three years, could they not have just left us alone? Patricia had changed her name to Laura, and she had dyed her hair and grown in long. She needed to do something to hide her identity so that she could lead some sort of life after the scandal. She never asked the newspaper photographer to take her picture, he did that anyway, as the police took Dara away in handcuffs. The picture captured the tears in her eyes even though it was reproduced in newsprint, the tracks were clear to see and her face showed her broken heart and fear.

Her life had not been at the glorious end of enjoyments. Her father had harmed her when she was but a tiny baby, social services could not leave her in such circumstances and so she became one of those babies that would rock themselves in their cot at night and bang their head on the cot end, with such vigour any nursery nurse would immediately consider concussion. She survived the nursery, Willow House, on The Rose Tree Estate, and she progressed her whole childhood on The Rose Tree Estate, moving from house to house as the years went by. They were good years for Patricia, she was a mild, likeable, child who could tell jokes, and who could be very cheeky. She smiled and she helped as much as she could, with all that she could.

In nineteen seventy-four Patricia was fifteen years old and a new house-parent came to work at Sycamore House. Patricia had never seen such a young man before. She felt her eyes drawn to watch him and she found it hard to avert her gaze. Dara did not notice Patricia any more than any of the other adolescent persons he was there to care for. In three weeks it was as if Dara had always been a part of the team. It was a good team, as near to a family as the circumstances would allow.

The daily routine was; everybody up, wash, brushed teeth, dressed and down for breakfast. Everyone sat at various tables in a large communal room, everyone had their place so there could not be arguments. All meals were preceded by a house-parent saying grace. Until it was said all would sit in silence, once the grace had been said people could eat and talk as they wished.

There had been discussions with a salesman who had offered to sell breakfast cereals to The Rose Tree Estate which would be the same as the products available in the shops but with plain packaging. This idea had been rejected by one, very clever, senior manager who said that it would be unwise to make the children of Rose Tree feel any more different from their peers who had the fortune to live in 'normal' family homes.

"I do not wish to alienate the children who live here any more than some of them feel already. They shall have the normal cereal boxes, it may only be a small thing, but the small things are often all that I can control around here."

The salesman was completely bemused; he thought that everything was about saving money.

When all the breakfast had been consumed there was another period of silence when notices were given. Then all would help to remove the empties from the tables and wipe them down, the floor would then be swept.

Then it was off to school for everyone. Sycamore House fell, more or less, silent for the day other than the sounds of vacuum cleaners working and noises from the kitchen. There were various meetings of social workers and people from the office. Then, around four in the afternoon, the young ones would return and they would change from their school clothes and do homework. Then it would be time for tea. That would be followed by games, inside or out depending on the weather. Cricket or football, table tennis or Monopoly. Some would gather about the record player and dance to the latest hits. As the evening wore on some would watch the television, sew, or knit.

Some would drift off to bed early; some would wait for a hot drink and a biscuit. Hot chocolate or malted milk, custard cream, digestive. Then they would brush their teeth again and be ready for lights out by ten.

Most of the time everyone was compliant, sometimes there were arguments, that was only to be expected. Most days were peaceful enough and most days, the distorted family life, which was Sycamore House, on The Rose Tree Estate was harmonious.

Illnesses were cared for by Matron. During Patricia's time at Sycamore House, there was a time when she and the other children felt secure and loved. Now that needs qualification because what is love? Love is, in this case, nothing to do with hugs, and kisses and holding hands. In this case in was mutual respect and feeling secure, being as happy as one could be under the circumstances. There was not much physical contact between staff and children, the occasional arm about the shoulder if Matron thought comfort was required, maybe to sooth after some tiff. Occasionally because someone had fallen through the cracks in the facade and realised for a moment or two that this life really was not as normal as people tried to make it out to be. There was not abuse, sexual or otherwise, at this time in Sycamore House within this group of people.

Patricia was now all but sixteen, indeed, it had been agreed that there would be a party in twenty-one days to mark her sixteenth year.

It was Dara who had been tasked with taking Patricia to the shops, for that was another part of life in a children's home, just as in any home, is that clothes are outgrown or ware out. So it was a trip to *Freeman Hardy and Willis*, in the high street for a new pair of school shoes for Patricia. The shoes would serve for school and would also be her birthday present.

Patricia, or Laura as she was now know, sat at the witness desk, behind the screen, she was well dressed in a pale pink dress with a matching short jacket. She had a single string of pearls about her neck and matching earrings. She had a handbag which was in perfect harmony with her outfit. The handbag matched her high heel shoes.

She sat upright in the chair her legs together and leaning slightly to the left. Her hair was light brown and had been styled.

The chairman invited Patricia to speak, but before any word could be heard she used a small linen handkerchief, embroidered with a rose, to dry a tear that had fallen from her right eye. Patricia had embroidered that rose, at Sycamore House, forty-four years before. It was something special to her, a reminder of a happy time when matron and other house-parents, would sit, and knit, and sew, and embroider whilst *Coronation Street* would playing on the black and white television.

Laura composed herself. Then she started to speak. What came from her was more surprising than anyone in that room had ever expected to hear.

"I am sixty years old, I have made a good life for myself, I have my own business and it is profitable. Part of my success I owe to the years I spent on The Rose Tree Estate. I went there as a baby, rescued from a violent father, and a mother who could not protect me from him. I do not remember them, but that is what I have been told. I have never married, I have loved only one man, and I love him to this day, and I will love him until the day I die."

Patricia reached for the glass of water that was on the table, and again dried her eye.

"I was fifteen when I first saw him, I found it hard to take my eyes away from him whenever he was near. He was kind, and gentle, and he knew such a lot about so many things. He was my hero, he was more than the father I had never had. He was truthful and compassionate and never once did he lay a finger on me, violently or sexually. He was not that sort of person."

Patricia paused for a moment and then continued.

"Oh I wanted him to touch me, in the night in my bed. I would fantasise that he was kissing me, and, if he had asked me for a kiss in real life, I would have gladly done so. Then just twenty-one days, before my sixteenth birthday he was assigned to take me to buy some new shoes. I was so excited. We went into town on the bus. There was little choice, I had to choose sensible brown shoes, they were for school as well as being my birthday present. He knew they had to be sensible school shoes too, but he allowed me to ask the sales girl to get several different pairs of fancy shoes from the stock room to try on. While we waited, he let me stand on the special foot-measuring machine, I could see my feet in the mirror. The sales assistant measured my feet on a wooden foot measure, with a sliding wooden bits and leather straps, you do not see those things any more. We went back to Sycamore House with my new brown shoes in a box, and the box in a big paper carrier bag marked *FHW*, the initials of the name of the shop, many people said it meant *For Happy Walking*.

Patricia paused for a few moments and coughed.

"You see when you have nothing much, anything simple is something extraordinary, and a pair of new shoes that were for me, and me alone, were special. I was further excited that I was buying them with a man I thought, at fifteen years of age, that I would marry. Yes, I was a daft little immature girl in those days. I did not understand the feelings I had, I only knew I had them -- and that I liked them.

"Life returned to normal and the twenty-one days disappeared, one by one, until the day I became sixteen. I knew that there was a cake, and people said happy birthday to me. I felt so good in my new shoes. Then as I left for school, I turned and there he was behind me, I moved closer, I went up on my tiptoes and I kissed him on the lips. I had never kissed anyone before. I was in love. It was so nice and it filled me with all good feelings".

Patricia paused

"That kiss ruined my life. I fear it ruined Dara's life too. Yet it was really nothing to do with him. It was all me. When I returned from school, Matron called me into her office and questioned me for an hour about

Dara. She asked if he had touched me and what had happened the day he went to the shop to buy my shoes. I told her that nothing had happened. I told her that I was sorry I had kissed him.

I was then allowed to go to my birthday celebrations. I remember blowing out the candles and the others sang *Happy Birthday,* but I really did not hear them The moment the candles were extinguished there was a great commotion. There were police, and Dara, was taken away. I have not seen him since. I came here today because I know that you are here to discuss some evil things that happened to many children and young people. I just had to come to publicly record that Dara did not do anything to harm me or, I am sure, anybody else, he was the sweetest man, and I love him even now and I am so, so sorry, for I am sure that I am responsible for ruining a good man's life, and I have lived with this burden for forty-four years and it burns me every day."

Patricia got up from her witness chair and left by the door at the back so that no one could see her face. The usher moved in to replace the glass of water and the screen was pulled back.

There were many other stories that day and many stories, which were written down and handed, posted, or emailed to the enquiry. Overall they painted a broad picture of the complex ecosystem that was The Rose Tree Estate and there were many glimpses of other, similar institutions. It started to become obvious that evil things had happened in many places, not just at Rose Tree.

It could not possibly be said that there was no 'bad behaviour', that there is just 'behaviour'. It cannot be debated that the bad behaviour was any more, or any less, on the side of house-parents or residents. However, it was obvious that house-parents were adults and any of them harming anyone in their care, could only be seen as committing a heinous crime.

As the stories were unpacked what did emerge most strongly was that although there were great examples of good care, fun, affection, laughter and all the things that make up a life. Sadly there were many adults who took advantage of children, and some adults did use some of the children for perverted sexual purposes. This led many children to suffer physical, and emotional harm which many had failed to cope with in the subsequent years. Now, at this enquiry, some of these people had been given a chance to speak. Sadly, those who had died would be forever silent.

It is sad to note that there were several suicides amongst those who had been harmed. Remember too, the harm, caused by a few, sullied the names of all those who worked as carers on The Rose Tree Estate. All the good that the decent people did was muted by the anguished cries of torment that was now let free from The Rose Tree Survivors.

Some weeks after the public hearings had begun the chairperson ordered that a record be made of all the good and positive things that did come out of The Rose Tree Estate. She appealed to those who were present, and to those others who had not been involved in the hearings, to come forward, not only with tales of awful harms but also with tales of good. So a 'good register' was set up citing the names of those house-parents who, it was agreed, had not caused harm. There was an objection to this list, a barrister cleared his throat and stood.

"I can understand why you have a desire to make such a list, however, we have heard tales of terrible harms and I have to ask the question, why did these so called good people not realise what was happening and put a stop to it?"

It was at this point in the proceedings that a woman in her middle fifties spoke. She was a thin woman, she wore spectacles which had thick black frames and that hid much of her small face. It was obvious that her clothes were not new and that they had seen better days.

"My name is Sandy McCann. I would like to try and answer the barrister's question if I may."

The chairperson asked Sandy to come to the front and Sandy sat at the witness table. What Sandy bought with her the atmosphere of a gospel church in America, where the congregation repeats the last bit of everything said by the preacher. Indeed, Sandy was a member of a big African Gospel Choir, she had been a member since 2002 when it had started.

"I was a resident of The Rose Tree Estate. I was not abused by anyone, however, I do know of two of my friends who did suffer. I can tell you their names and I can tell you who harmed them. The man did not touch me, he preferred girls whose skin was of a lighter shade than mine. He told me once just how much he detested my colour. I did not know about his abuse until after the three of us had left The Rose Tree Estate. I have to say that I was totally shocked when they told me what had happened. The power this man had over my friends was quite extraordinary, they lived in fear of him. They would never have told anyone whilst they were there, for fear of what he might do to them. Both had come to The Rose Tree Estate from appalling circumstances. Dirty, rat-infested homes where they had been abused, one by her father, the other by her uncle. To go back to the life they had had before Rose Tree was more than they could bear. They both, independently, decided that it was far better to endure the sex with this house-parent rather than have to return to filth, hunger and abuse from their relatives. You see, stories are always multi-layered, there are many reasons that people do things and I can tell you that my friends considered it the price they had to pay for being safe, clean, fed, and warm. At home they had had none of these luxuries, but they did have the abuse. The men, and I now know there were women involved too, who took advantage of children on Rose Tree, never did anything to cause suspicion. There were many places on Rose Tree and in the big houses where any type of activity could go on without witness. There were plenty of locked doors with spaces behind. There were plenty of vulnerable young people, many of whom knew nothing of sex, and many thought that sex with someone older than themselves was normal. Having said that, the majority, like myself, were never preyed upon. I am prepared to write down the names of my friends and the name of the man who abused them. I will not say their names openly, for although I know for certain what I had said is the truth, these people are not present and I do not have their permission to reveal their names. It should be for the police to investigate and seek justice, although I am happy to testify on behalf of my friends for they suffered terrible harm.

Chapter 38
Ceylon.
Narrator

"No that is not what I can say, I really do not think you know very much about the reality of life. Have you ever considered that, perhaps, your life experience is a bit shallow to be a reporter? How old are you anyway?" Said Desmond.

Desmond was born in England. His parents had emigrated from Ceylon in nineteen forty-eight when Ceylon had become independent of the British Empire. They found that England could be cold and inhospitable to people of their skin tone. They kept themselves to themselves. Desmond's father started an import-export business and often travelled. He was successful, in eight years his business was big enough for the family to move to a beautiful house in the Surrey countryside. Then, as the autumn of nineteen fifty-nine arrived, Desmond's father had a business trip; he boarded a *British Overseas Airways Corporation Britannia 312* aeroplane to travel to Hong Kong, some called this aircraft The Whispering Giant. Asian Flu had caused many deaths in the previous two years; indeed, there had been over five hundred deaths in England and Wales. Unfortunately Desmond's father caught it, he succumbed to pneumonia, and died. Desmond's mother was devastated by this tragedy; Desmond was just two years old.

It was a complete, and horrific, surprise when Desmond's mother died; Desmond was never given an explanation as to what caused the second tragedy. It was the tragedy that ultimately led Desmond to The Rose Tree Estate. He was too young to remember, and really it was the first home he knew.

Desmond continued. "If that is what you think about The Rose Tree Estate, all I can say about your research is that it really is not up to much!

I was on the Estate from before I can remember until I left school when I was sixteen. Nineteen fifty-nine until nineteen seventy-three. What exactly would have happened to me, or all the other children and young people who lived there?

I was an orphan, with brown skin, dark hair, and brown eyes. I had no one to care for me. Yes of course some things were difficult but at least I was not dead! Yes there were a few funny men who liked little boys. They were not only house-parents, there were also local councillors, for example, who took special interest, the occasional tradesman, and I was even once propositioned by a policemen!

I really am not approving or condoning what any of these people did. I do know the awful harm that was caused to many of my Rose Tree brothers and sisters.

However, it was not always a one-way traffic. For some of the girls and boys, what shall I say? The molestations were a substitute for the lack of love and physical contact they did not have from elsewhere, so they accepted them as a trade-off. There were those, I am not saying this was all, far from it, but there were those who did use it as a trade-off for something that they wanted, or needed, extra privilege, some extra food, maybe some money whatever, it was, a little sexual activity was one way for them to get what they wanted.

On occasions, I think, there were even some genuine exchanges of love.

It's a complex business. The Rose Tree Estate was a reflection of the world, and it was it's own world. There were many children who were never approached by...what's the term they use nowadays? Oh yes, the pedos. In that group there were some who wished to be approached, and others who felt bad that they were not approached. There were others who never knew, or thought about, such things, I would say they were the majority. As I said, I know many who were definitely harmed very deeply by these things.

I suppose they way some looked at it as a small price to pay for having a warm place to sleep and some food.

Once I had worked it out I made a business of it. I was told my dad had been a businessman, well maybe I inherited that gene. When I left The Rose Tree Estate, at the age of sixteen in nineteen seventy-three, I had a bank account that contained over eight thousand pounds. The average wage then was not twenty pounds per week! I had nearly eight years of average pay in the bank at the age of sixteen.

Most of that I got for letting some guy, or another, touch my prick whilst he rubbed himself off.

It was all about making the best of the situation, some could, others couldn't.

Now I am not gay, and I am happily married with four beautiful children. I will do all in my power to keep my children from paedophiles, and from the circumstances that I had to survive. However, I feel no malice towards any of the men who touched me, there were a couple of women too, and one older boy from Hornbeam House, on the Rose Tree. The warden of Hornbeam House was a monster, Archibald Anderson was his name, he did something to that young lad that made him really weird. Not many are born to a royal households, with servants, and food, and clothes and money. Survival is not easy; some people do better than others. So write your piece but remember when you do so that not all the children of Rose Tree were victims, although I weep for those who were.

For me Rose Tree was mother and father, and it set me on a path of success. I have no complains to make, I will be forever be grateful for what it did for me.

The reporter closed his notebook; he looked exasperated, and said:

"I can't use any of that, that's not what the readers expect!"

Chapter 39
Barry and the Run-Away's.
Narrator

"Oh heavens and all damnation!" exclaimed an exasperated Barry, Warden of Pine Lodge, on The Rose Tree Estate, as he put down the telephone receiver. The Matron, Marion Forbes, looked over at Barry and asked:

"What is the bother Barry?" Barry responded:

"Tina and Monica, the police have found them, they are at the South End on Sea police station!"

Marion looked shocked: "How on earth did they manage to get that far away from here? You have to hand it to them, that is a long way to get to with no money!"

Barry said: "Yes I know. Now it looks as if I will have to go up there and get them. We really have not have the staff available today. Marion you will have to hold the fort. I will ring the social work office, I'll need a female with me, and I do hope they have someone who is actually good at the job to send with me."

A couple of hours later and Barry was in the back of a taxi. The social worker that had been provided by the social work office was sitting in the front seat next to the driver. The driver smoked one cigarette after another, throwing each dog-end from the open window. To say it was a ramshackle old car would be being nice. Barry could not help but notice that the speedometer did not work.

They entered the Dartford Tunnel, it was a hot summer day, sweat soaked Barry's shirt in the armpits and rested on his brow. The driver would not put up his window so the fumes from the other vehicles were invading Barry's lungs. He was asthmatic and the smoke from the driver's constant puffing and the fumes, combined, made him feel miserable. His thought was they could not even send me in a decent car.

The police sergeant at the desk in Southend-on-Sea police station, said to Barry and Wendy, the social worker:

"Boy I am glad to see you. How on earth do you look after these two?" The sergeant led the way to the cells, and there, caged behind the bars one might have seen on a cowboy movie, were Tina, aged twelve, and Monica, age thirteen. Tina was the leader. They were shouting and screaming. Then they saw Barry and they started to laugh as well. The police sergeant handed Barry a clipboard and asked Barry to sign a document to indicate the girls were no longer in the care of the police. He then pulled a truncheon from the wasteband on his trousers and he bashed the metal bars with it. He shouted in a voice that was as the roar of a walrus in battle. The girls were visibly shaken by the intensity of the cry. He told them to close their mouths on pain of being taken before the magistrate. Barry was unsure if they would understand what a magistrate was but Tina said: "Watch it copper, we ain't dun nuffing that no magistrate is interested in."

Barry stared at both the girls and somehow their bravado slid away. They obediently followed him out of the police station and climbed into the taxi. Wendy said that it was not possible for her to sit in the back with the two girls because she would get carsick if she travelled in the back. Barry thought, 'what a waste of a salary this woman is.' He had worked with her before, and this trip had not improved the impression he had of her.

It was an awful return journey, late afternoon, hot summer sun, Friday afternoon traffic building into the rush hour, and worse, a traffic jam in the Dartford Tunnel. Tina and Monica felt hot and they were thirsty. They kept asking for a drink. Then they wanted to go to the toilet. Barry did his best to keep them calm. The girls felt kind of good that they had got all this attention. They knew that they had got under the skin of the police in Southend-on-Sea, however, they had not expected this taxi ride and had no plans as to what they could do to disrupt it. They did have a code word they used it to distract people's attention. It had often been useful, including once when they were nearly caught shoplifting.

Tina said: "Bull-Dog."

Suddenly, in the middle of that hot, dark, smelly, Dartford Tunnel, with Barry in the middle, Tina and

Monica started a scrap. They were shouting at each other and throwing punches.

Barry said: "Wendy help." She did nothing. Barry tried to grab Tina's wrist. He managed instead to catch a grip on Monica and took a forceful punch on his cheek from Tina, for his trouble. Monica reached over with her other hand and pulled a handful of hair from Barry's head, Tina joined in and took a handful from the other side. The fight seemed to go on forever. Then suddenly there was a pause and both girls opened the taxi doors, just at the moment the taxi jolted forward and started to move again after the eternity of being stationary.

Years later when his own children asked him why he had gone bald Barry told them this story. His children laughed and told him that the story could not be true and that he was an 'Old Sprucer'.

*

The Rose Tree Estate provided opportunities for many different kinds relationships. There were jealousies between children. There were notable times when children would gang-up against a house-parent. There were even times when house-parents ganged up against other house-parents. It was a complex and difficult 'universe' to explore and to navigate. Some were able to others were not.

*

Chapter 40

The Police Constables Note Book.

Narrator

When I arrived on the scene, on The Rose Tree Estate, Elm House, eighteen hundred hours Saturday, fifth June, nineteen seventy-six, things looked pretty difficult. A teenage girl, Rebecca Jordan, date of birth; fourteenth of August, nineteen sixty-three, current age, thirteen years old, had a broken bottle in her hand. She was waving it in the air and threatening to lunge the jagged glass at a male house-parent, Howard Rushworth, date of birth fifteenth of May, nineteen forty-one, thirty-five years old. A large group of teenage girls had gathered around Rebecca Jordan and were encouraging her with chanting. They used explicit language. It was a particularly ugly scene. I managed to push my way to the front of the crowd and to the right of Rebecca Jordan, I swivelled around in the space between her and Howard Rushworth. I managed to grasp Rebecca Jordan's right hand with my left hand as she lunged forward to slash Howard Rushworth. I could easily have been a second too late. My action certainly prevented an injury to Howard Rushworth. This was my fourth visit to this care home in one week. There had been incidents involving three other teenage girls and other staff members on second, third and fourth of the month. Notes about these incidents occur on previous pages in this notebook. To recap, on Tuesday one teenage girl emptied a jug of hot gravy over the head of a female house-parent. On Wednesday another girl threatened a male house-parent with a knife. On Thursday another teenage girl squirted washing up liquid into the eyes if another female house-parent. There has been a week of violence. I discovered that the teenage girls have been listening to the police frequency on a radio. None of the house-parents were prepared to bring charges. I have asked that the staff at Elm House confiscate the radio. I have agreed to attend a meeting of staff and social workers to discuss what steps can be taken to restore the peace at Elm House

I was called to The Rose Tree Estate, Elm House, at eighteen hundred hours, Monday seventh June, nineteen seventy-six. When I arrived the Fire Service were in attendance. The disused toilet block, behind Elm House, was ablaze. I, and other officers, took statements from all the residents and house-parents. I discovered an empty *Tizer* bottle which smelt as if petrol had been carried in it. According to the chief fireman, the blaze was started deliberately. I am in an on-going investigation to discover who was responsible for the arson.

*

It was the first week of December, nineteen seventy-six when Rebecca found herself in the Crown Court. She was fourteen years of age now. Her life had not started well, a catalogue of misfortune and misadventure had claimed all the days from her birth until the age of seven when she first came to The Rose Tree Estate. Her little arms were thin and her dark brown skin had the scars of burns made by cigarettes that had been extinguished upon her by her stepfather. The stepfather and her ineffectual mother had died in a car accident in nineteen fifty-nine. There were different opinions expressed as to whether or not she had been lucky to survive. Her injuries left deep scars on her face and she had suffered some damage to her brain.

So much had happened to Rebecca, and so much of it was unkind. She had never asked to be born; yet here she was. This is what she knew, and somehow she knew it was all wrong, from the pain of the cigarette burns and the lashings of the belt the man had hit her with to being so hungry and thirsty and so, so cold. Not only that, he had stopped her mother from cuddling her, so it was hardly much of a story to see that Rebecca had some scores to settle with the life into which she had been thrust.

Some of the kids at school taunted her for the colour of her skin and the marks on her face. Before the accident and before The Rose Tree Estate, they called her 'Smelly Becca'; they ribbed her about her threadbare clothes.

Now that she was in trouble with the law she had grown a bristling network of sharp thorns about her and she told herself she did not care what anybody did to her. She vowed she would remember and one day she would get them back; the children who taunted and the adults who did not see the hurt she had endured. Her resentment extended to the police who just compounded, and made worse, everything that had already happened in her life. Now she faced this judge and jury; who were they to understand the protest she had made? Maybe they saw through all of this and knew that in Rebecca's plan to set fire to the toilet block was merely a practice run for the distruction of Elm House itself and all the inhabitants. Although she had no written plan, the plan was in her head.

You cannot comprehend the deep, dark, hurt in the hearts of some who never asked to be born, and have never been shown a good way; the way to survive and thrive. To give something, you have to first possess it. All that Rebecca had to give was the bile and evil she had received during her short time on Earth.

Nonetheless, Rebecca was sent to borstal by the judge. His judgment came to Rebecca in the voice tones of the privileged; listening to his, so-called, cultured voice, Rebecca could have been hearing Chinese Mandarin for all the sense he made. From where she was, the world made no sense at all. She had watched television, she had seen what other people do, and have, and she knew her life had been so different -- and now this! What was this? You do not get a positive by adding to negatives, at least that is what that maths teacher had told the class.

Chapter 41
Session Thirteen: Enquiry
Kristopher

Doctor Samuels was the first to speak. He asked me a question. "Have you been following the enquiry Kristopher? What do you make of it all?"

I thought about his question for a while, and then I said: "Well, some of the stories are all but unbelievable, yet I am convinced that I have heard no lies. It seems to me that The Rose Tree Estate was a sort of living being, some sort of organism, which although attached to the rest of the world was, at the same time, apart from the world. A little universe of it's own. There were obviously some very good people amongst the staff and then there were those who took advantage of the situation for their own gratification without any thought that their actions would have awful consequences for the lives of so many."

I fidgeted on my seat for a moment as a chill came over me. I think for the first time in my life I truly realised just how fortunate I had been in having a loving dad and mum, and how desperate it must have been for most of the young people who came to The

Rose Tree Estate. How confused, and how lonely some, maybe all, of them were. I thought how I was free to roam about the place; yet as far as I could remember, no one ever did me harm. Why? There would have been plenty of opportunities; I was so often alone, I did wander all over the estate on my tricycle. At this point in my thoughts I could feel that there was something that I was trying to remember, something from the locked cages that Doctor Samuels had been trying to tease out of me during the previous twelve sessions. The sessions so far totalled twenty-four hours of my life, recalling what would have been a time span of a few years. Time is a tricky thing, it bends and snakes into corners, and then, like a rainbow, it breaks into a spectrum of unexpected cascades of tiny remembrances and even when all of this had been done there was still a little bit in the corner, a little bit that cannot wash out, or that I could get a grip on.

"I was so, so lucky to have parents who cared for me, loved me and set me up on the road, with rules, manners, a code to live by, and self-confidence. Is that the thing self-confidence? Is that the thing that the children who were prayed upon lacked? After all why should they have had any confidence at all?"

"Being unable to control what happens to your own body, is that one of the most frightening things there is?"

"Kristopher." Spoke the Doctor as another shiver descended my spine, I woke from the trance of words that had just come from me. The doctor continued:

"Kristopher, during the session before last, you told me of the dreams you used to have whilst staying at your granny's house. Have you been able to think any more about those dreams?"

I replied: "Well I have tried, but all that I can remember is what I told you before. I have decided to go along and sit in on some of the sessions of the enquiry. I will tell you about the experience in two weeks."

Chapter 42
Written Evidence
Narrator

Desmond had been working at Ash House for six months. He started his work shortly after the new year in nineteen seventy-two. Coming to Ash House was an eye-opener for Desmond.

Desmond had had a privileged start in life; his father had a good business producing flavourings for food products. The business supplied food manufactures with a huge range of different products. Desmond had five sisters and a brother, he was the middle child. They lived in a very nice house, with mock Tudor wooden beams, a driveway and plenty of space for this large family. It was a house full of love and all necessary comforts were available. Although Desmond had been to a private school, his final marks were not up to the standard required for university, in fact they fell well short. Desmond's father decided that a spell in the local further education college might be a good step, so it was arranged and Desmond found himself on retake courses. He did well and Desmond's father found a junior management position in the company for him. Desmond spent some time in the United States of America, and upon his return, his father said to him that it might be good to experience the lives of people who had not been born into such a privileged life. Hence Desmond's appointment as a house-parent on The Rose Tree Estate.

It came as a shock at first, violent acts between the young people in Ash House were frequent. In his first week there was an incident where one teenage girl picked up a large water jug and clonked it down onto the head of another girl. The attack came without warning and right in front of his eyes. There was blood all over the place and before much time had passed he was in the back of ambulance escorting the injured girl to the hospital. Several hours later, his white shirt crimson with blood, a taxi took them back to Ash House.

Desmond was on a night duty, sleeping in the staff bedroom, available to respond if something happened. Nothing had happened on all the other nights he had done this, but on one night there was a banging on the door and a short, ginger-haired girl, who had freckles and who was a bit overweight, was seated on the floor in the corridor. She was nursing a foot which had a huge cut in the sole of the heal. Desmond wiped around the wound and bandaged it. He called at the door of one of the live-in staff and explained he would need to take the girl to causality. It was about three o'clock in the morning when they arrived at the hospital. The hospital was quiet and the nurse examined the foot and asked the girl why she had gone into the garden at night with no shoes on her feet. The girl just looked over the nurse's shoulder and said nothing. It was necessary to x-ray the foot. By the time all this was done, it was about five o'clock in the morning. When the nurse looked at the x-ray she was stunned. She became very angry with the girl and asked her how on earth the girl had managed to push a paper clip, round side, into her own foot. The girl just stared into space. The nurse then called the x-ray department to confirm what the nurse had seen on the x-ray. She laughed and put down the phone.

"I am sorry." She said. " I should not have accused you. The radiologist just told me he had run out of markers to show where foreign materials may have entered the wound, so he used a paper clip instead. Thank goodness for that, I really thought we would be dealing with a big problem."

It is eight o'clock in the morning when they arrived back at Ash House. The girl, Penny, had to rest in bed until the stitches could be removed.

Desmond went home to sleep, his father and his mother often wondered if the stories he told them of Ash House, on The Rose Tree Estate, were true or if he made them up.

It was not an easy thing to work in Ash House, but at the end of a year Desmond had learned so much about people, he was truly grateful for the experience. Although there were many difficult moments during that year, there were many happy moments too that he would always cherish.

Chapter 43
Judge
Narrator

Judge Amoy MacCree, was of Jamaican decent, She was a puisne, or ordinary, Judge and was well respected by all who knew her, she commanded a good reputation. Her staff were all but overwhelmed by the sheer volume of written submissions that came to them. Each was carefully read, logged and filed. Each person who wrote to the enquiry received a written response.

Beverly Crowthorne was a woman in her mid-forties, she had raised her children and, after a break of several years, was preparing to return to work at a firm of solicitors when she was invited to be interviewed for a position as a part of the enquiry team. She passed the interview and accepted the new role. A couple of weeks into the job and she confided in her husband.

"I really cannot go into detail, or tell you about the work, I just did not expect the stories I have to deal with to be so harrowing. While I am doing this job, Peter, I will need a lot of support from you, and I will need your understanding. Some of the stuff I have already come across would make you cry, I cannot believe some of the things that happened to these tiny human beings. Suppose something had happened to us and our three had ended up in that system. Oh Peter, it is absolutely ghastly."

Here are some exerpts from some of the letters and emails which Beverly read:

1 "There was a man who came to give piano lessons, he would insist on leaning our me from behind and placing his hands on mine, he would direct my fingers. Each time he pulled away he would brush my breasts. On the occasion which upset me the most, I felt him squeeze me tight to him, I could feel him on my back, he was erect, he leaned over and touched me between my legs. I will never erase that memory. Then he told me not to worry, it was just something he did with his extra special pupils. He said I should not say anything in case I should find myself in trouble for not

doing my piano homework. I never did master the piano, and I cannot listen to the sound of one, without feeling that man's breath, panting in my ear."

2 "Until that moment I did not know things could go up it! To me it was just where my poo came out, now I was pinned down by two men whilst the third pushed his thing into me. I was like a lighted match and it hurt me and left me very sore, there was blood on my underwear when I undressed for bed. He told me that no one would believe me if I told them what he had done, besides, he said, these two friends of mine will call you out as a liar if you should say anything."

3 "It never happened to me, I do not know why. After lights-out she would come into the dormitory. She would rouse one of my fellows and lead them, by the hand, out of the darkness and down the corridor. No one would speak of what had happened. Then a new girl arrived, she told me that she thought she had had a dream, a dream in which she had been taken to a bathroom, a women had taken off all her clothes and then removed the new girl's nightdress. Then the two got into the bath together and the women wanted the new girl to wash her with a bar of soap. The new girl was told where she had to rub."

There where many tales from many people, most had been residents on The Rose Tree Estate in the nineteen seventies and nineteen eighties. There was one from the late nineteen fifties. This testimony was delivered in person:

"It seems so long ago now, I still have difficulty in grasping everything that went on all those years ago. I was quite small and I was in this place for a short time. What flashes through my memory is a warm sunny day with blue sky. I went for a little wander about on The Rose Tree Estate. I got myself lost; I was not sure how to find my way back to my house. It was a special day, there was a big sports event. The grounds were extensive and I was quite a small child. I came across a place which was for growing vegetables. There where greenhouses, water butts and many rows of vegetables, salad plants and herbs. There was a grass strip between two of the greenhouses. I could hear some panting sounds and I peered around the edge of one greenhouse and I saw the back of a man and a fat women, who was naked, she was lying on a blanket on the grass. There was a tricycle by the wall of the other greenhouse, and there was a little boy who was also naked. The whole scene frightened me and I did not know what to do. I stood still for a moment, staring at the back of the man. Then it seemed as though he was about to turn around, I thought maybe he had heard me. I turned and ran away as fast as I could. Maybe the fear of what that man might have done to me, if he had caught me, was enough to make me remember the way back to my house. I never saw them again, I do not know who they were, or exactly what they were doing. For all I know they have been a married couple with their child and she was sun bathing in the nude. However, that was not the feeling I had at the time, and it is not the feeling I have about it now. All these years I have, from time to time, thought about that incident, I have wondered who that little boy was, if he was the child of this couple. You see in the late nineteen-fifties taking all your clothes off outdoors, was a very rare occurrence indeed, even in high summer. Even after all these years, I really do not know what to make of it. Possibly I am wasting your time with a half-baked story."

Judge Amoy MacCree said: "You are surely not wasting our time Mr. Phelps. Your story has been recorded and may well be used to complete, or add to, some other stories, which have, or may be contributed. This enquiry thanks you very much for your time and for your courage in speaking out."

Mr. Phelps replied: "Please may I just say something else?"

"Of course you may." Said the Judge.

"I owe my life to The Rose Tree Estate, I would have surely died if I had not been taken there by the police. My stay there was not too long because I was fostered and later adopted. My memory of Rose Tree was that people were kind to me, I was warm, I was clean, I was fed and there was a bed that was mine. All that we have been hearing about; some of the dreadful things which went on there; well it is shocking to me. Apart from the story I have told to you, I knew nothing of anything untoward, and I wish I could say thank you to those who were kind to me all those years ago. There had been little kindness in my life before I went there."

Mr. Phelps stood up and went back into the body of the crowd and sat once again in the 'audience'.

Chapter 44
Session Fourteen: Nettles
Kristopher

"You know for all I said about my freedoms when I was a youngster there was one incident in my childhood when I nearly died. They had a huge coal fire in the back of the garage; it had to be kept going twenty-four hours a day, to heat the house and the hot water. There was a huge top-loading, washing machine and the water it required was put into it by attaching a hose to the hot water tap and dangling it into the machine. The water was all but boiling as it came from the tap. I was on my own, as usual, dad and mum had gone out, they told me that if I needed anything one of the staff would help me. I watched as the member of staff started doing the washing. As the water filled the machine, the hose jumped up, there must have been a surge of water. The scalding hot water splashed up and fell all over me. I must have been unconscious for I remember nothing until I woke up in a bed. I was lying on my back and I had paraffin gauze sheets, sticky-brown, loosely-woven laid all over my chest. It hurt and I remained in bed for a long time, daily visits from the doctor, or a nurse were arranged. It must have been six weeks or more before I recovered."

"Another time I got the measles. That nearly did for me too. I remember I was at granny's house when that happened, the curtains were drawn, they were blackout curtains left over from the war, they made the room dark as a coal cellar. I remember little from this time except being blind due to my eyes being gummed together with mucus. I remember needing to go to the toilet. Granny found me lying on the floor under the bathroom sink. I thought I was standing up going to the toilet. My grandparent's generation had a very different view of illness; they had lived through half a century before the National Health Service came about. Granny often recalled having her tonsils removed, without anaesthetic, whilst laying on the kitchen table."

Dr. Samuels asked: "How are these stories relevant to that which has been going on in the enquiry Kristopher?"

I replied: "Well I am not the only person to have experienced a near death. I was looked after and cared for and I survived. I was cared for but I felt very scared, I had loving parents, and grandparents, but still I felt very much alone. There were many hours which I spent on my own in a bedroom or around the estate. What must it have been like for the poor young children on The Rose Tree Estate? Those orphans, those without someone to love and care for them. What happened if those little ones got ill?"

"There was an horrific story from one man in the enquiry. He spoke of a time when he was a teenager on The Rose Tree Estate and he was ill so the matron sent him to his bed. A doctor arrived, not the usual doctor. It seems that that man took advantage of an empty dormitory to examine the poor young fellow intimately. The man said that she thought that what the doctor had done was not nice but he had explained to him that it was a normal procedure when checking for mumps. He said that years later, when his own child had the mumps, and the doctor undertook an examination and he did not do what the other doctor had done to him. It was only then that he realised what had happened to him. He said that he felt so stupid and ashamed. Then he felt anger and that is what had brought him to the enquiry.

Then he started on the next part of his story. He said that there was a boy in Ash House known to everyone as Joe Slow, he to had had the mumps and he too had been examined by the same doctor. The man told the enquiry he had heard Joe Slow call out. 'Get your hands off me!' Then I heard his voice sound stifled, I imagined that the doctor had covered Joe's mouth with his hand, to stop him alerting a member of staff. Then the Judge asked the man why the doctor was alone, was there not a member of staff with him? The man responded saying:

"'Of course not they were all busy, they would never have dreamed of accompanying a doctor about the place. Joe was never quite right after that, I heard him talking to himself one day. 'That's what they do, grown ups, touch, always touching. They ain't touching me no more.' It wasn't long after that that Joe murdered Evelynn and put her in the dustbin.'"

"The man, once started, could not hold back his tears, the usher led him out of the enquiry room."

"When people are hurting inside they often hurt others. I was a victim of such. There were two girls on The Rose Tree Estate who were twins. They were not alike. One was taller than the other; one had darker hair than the other. I was going about my business, doing the things that I did to amuse myself, and they came over and started to talk with me. They said that they wanted to play. We ran about and played tag. During the game, we moved across the grass towards a big tree which had stinging nettles growing around the bottom of it. When we were very close to the nettles, the two girls turned on me, they grabbed my arms and pushed me into the nettles. I was stung from top to toe. It was a gruesome experience that I can feel to this moment. My dad was so cross when he discovered what had happened. He did something that, in a different time, may well have lost him his job. He pushed the girls into the nettles. It was a different world then. If this is to be judged it should be judged not by the taboos of now, but by the situation that pertained then. I will tell you that those girls did nothing to me again, nor did anyone else who heard this story."

"Doctor Samuels, the amount of terrible stories I have listened to at this enquiry freezes me as if I had been left at the North Pole in my swimming trunks. There was one man who testified that the priest, who was a regular visitor to The Rose Tree Estate, often slipped his hand down the back of his trousers. He said the priest would cross himself and then say out aloud: 'This is the work of the Lord.' He would then fumble about pushing his hand down, between the elasticated band, at the back of his trousers so that the palm of the priest's hand was flat against the skin of his bottom. The priest's hand would go right down and between his legs until he felt the priest's fingers on his testicles. At the time, at the age of eight, the man told the enquiry that he thought this was what happened in church things, in the name of the Lord!"

Chapter 45
The Prime Minister
Narrator

Daily updates from the enquiry arrived her red box. She noted that the ice cream van was, at least one joyful moment in the lives of torment that many children seemed to have lived on Rose Tree. A *'Strawberry Mivvi'* was a treat, it seems, for some. Claudia Kemsing, now Prime Minister, looked at the numbers, it seemed to her that even though those who were abused were many, there were still many more who were, more or less, un-harmed by their experience, of living on The Rose Tree Estate.

Tory prime ministers understand numbers. Numbers are easy. If you have one, and you get another one, now you have two. That is arithmetic everybody can get that. However, if we push on into mathematics we get percentages these are a very useful tool for any aspiring politician. In these types of numbers can be hidden all manor of nasty things. Claudia said to herself 'well if as many as twenty percent had some awful sexual molestation it still means that eighty per cent, the majority, had no bother at all'. If you were one of the twenty, yes twenty, in a hundred, in Claudia's calculation, would the fact that another eighty people, in your hundred, were not abused, give you much comfort? I think not. Claudia tried hard to sell this idea to herself – 'it was bad, but not all bad'. The truth is, no one can make up a sum to calculate the pain that was inflicted upon so many.

Claudia was trying to work out the arithmetic that could turn such pain into monetary compensation for the victims, and exactly what the chancellor would say to any proposed settlement amounts. Then she came to a story about one of her contemporary politicians. Someone she had been to university with, someone she had called 'friend' and someone she knew who had appeared in the documents she had arranged destroyed a while ago.

The man had had a life in politics, upon leaving university he progressed, more or less, straight into his local council. There he served as the youngest elected member ever. He was successful and was re-elected. Later his ambitions made him seek out a parliamentary seat. During his time on the council, he had always managed to be appointed to the committees which dealt with children. Claudia knew he was a frequent visitor to children's homes and schools, and now, Claudia read, his name had been bought to the attention of the enquiry. The evidence was damming, the pain this person had caused to many children on The Rose Tree Estate was quite simply horrific. The following morning it was headline news on radio, television and the Internet 'arrested and hauled away in a police car'. The pictures flooded the television screens of the nation, finishing with an image of his wife looking totally bemused and lost.

Claudia did not, for one second, believe that she had done the wrong thing by having those papers destroyed, she knew he could have been bought to justice long ago, but she also knew that he could have been blackmailed into many corners with the information she had, and that the information was just to valuable to just throw away. That particular advantage, for Claudia, vanished with his arrest, the paperwork that she was privy to was no more, so nothing could be laid at her door, she felt it was a shame that she had lost such an asset, but that is the way it goes. There was bound to be some up-coming young politician who would make some similar stupid mistake, sooner or later, and she would be there to catalogue and record it all, and then she would follow through, so she could control whoever it turned out to be. She sometimes felt spider like, capturing unsuspecting little politicians, so she could manipulate their actions, and votes, in her preferred direction. After all the politician who had enough compliant underlings in dependency would ultimately get the top job, which is, secretly, what she had always wanted. She never let her ambitions show, but she was the most ambitious politician of her generation. Home Secretary was not to far from Number Ten, and she had always known that that was her ultimate destination. The fact that she had deliberately kept quiet about his man and the suffering of former residents, of The Rose Tree Estate, really meant little to Claudia, whose deep thought was; 'what is all the fuss about? These kids were housed, fed, and clothed at the expense of the state, and he was so easy to manipulate.'

Chapter 46
Election
Narrator

Claudia thought she was very clever to announce an early General Election, even though the new 'Fix Term Parliament Act' was in force. She had enough support to get a two-thirds majority because the opposition parties were united in their distaste both of Claudia and her Government, this was their chance to have a go at taking control.

The campaign was short, dark, and messy. Policies not thought through, outlandish proposals, and various other shortcomings. Then at the enquiry a witness suggested, that whilst in the office of Home Secretary, Claudia Kemsing had ordered papers to be destroyed that proved that there had been people in government who had been involved in the abuse of children. A member of the cleaning staff at the Home Office, had found a couple of sheets of paper which had fallen behind the shredding machine and she had glanced through the first paragraph to see if the paper was important.

The story blistered across social media, television, radio and newspapers. Like the former Labour prime minister whose 'bigot' comment cost him his place in Ten Downing Street, this revelation ripped Claudia Kemsing from office and set police officers asking questions regarding the legality of Claudia's actions.

Chapter 47
House-Parent June
Narrator

June stood up and walked over to the chair where she was to give her evidence. June had written many books about childcare. She had trained as a nursery nurse whilst working at Willow House on the Rose Tree Estate in the early nineteen seventies. She was dressed in a smart, grey, two-piece suit with a white blouse.

"I should like to say that I worked for many years on The Rose Tree Estate and I, and many of my colleagues, I would say ninety-nine percent, loved their work. We were totally dedicated to the well-being of the children in our care. I know that I, and many others, tried to see the world from the perspective of the children in our care. We knew that it was not possible to substitute for a family and a home, but most of us worked tirelessly for the well-being of those for whom we cared."

"In my time, and in my experience, of The Rose Tree Estate, there were old stories, and rumours, of a visiting politician who had, it was said, taken advantage of some children. There was also some controversy over a laundry assistant. Those things were before my time. I became aware of the incident, which was described in this roo, a short time ago where a fifteen-year-old girl had kissed a house-parent. The man was instantly dismissed. Until I heard the witness here, I did not know any more of that incident."

"I have to say that some of what I have heard in this room, has moved me so much. I feel so sorry that witnesses here went through such horrific experiences. I will say it is my belief that most adults working with children on The Rose Tree Estate were not people who would do harm to anyone, let alone, those they were charged to care for."

"I am sure they; I am trying to speak for most house-parents when I say if any of us had noticed anything untoward, we would have reported it. I honestly knew of no such incidents."

Chapter 48
Café at Lunch Time
Narrator

Two men sat in a café, not far from where the enquiry was being held. It was lunchtime and the men had each ordered a pie and chips and a cup of tea.

"You see Terry we have been sitting in the enquiry listening to some shocking revelalations. You and I were both residents on The Rose Tree Estate at about the same time. We both remember some of the same people who were there, but we never met each other at the time."

Terry spoke: "That's right Barry, and of course we have 'him' in common, 'Daniel Evesham'." They fell silent for a moment. Terry was about to speak but the pie and chips arrived at their table. He continued: "What I really want to know is who interviewed that man for the job and did they not know about him? Surely there must have been some checks. Besides, he always created such an odd atmosphere whenever he came into a room. How was it that no one saw that before they gave him the job?"

Barry answered: "I cannot."

Terry cut Barry short: "Barry you know right well why no one ever said anything, you as I, along with many others, were absolutely terrified of him. That's the bit I really don't get -- how he could come across as nice to the general population and yet he was able to make our lives absolute hell."

"Well I think something should be done about those who gave him the job in the first place."

Terry said: "Well the bother with that Barry is they are all probably dead by now, Evesham had been working on The Rose Tree Estate long before we were there. Evesham is an old man now, and I wonder if anyone will be able to do anything about that bastard."

Barry said: "Drink up Terry we need to get back, we don't want to be late."

Chapter 49
Remember Grace?
Narrator

We met Grace earlier in this tale of The Rose Tree Estate. The Rose Tree Estate was different for each individual who became a part of it.

For Mr. Solms, the head-gardener, it was the most glorious of places. He loved to mow the lawns into stripes and fill the flowerbeds with colour and fragrance. He loved presenting the various cooks of Rose Tree with the fabulous vegetables, and salads that he and his men produced. There were apple trees and currant bushes. He also grew prize winning marrows.

"Who else, in these parts have fabulous, old fashioned greenhouses?" Mr. Solms asked his wife.

Mr. Sloms did get upset if sometimes the children, by mistake or through malicious intent, damaged any of his work, but he knew that it probably was not really their fault. Many of these young souls had had such a poor start in life.

Michelle had come from the West Indies, and she was a cook and she loved her job. She came from a big family and so cooking at Fern Tree House was simply like being at home. The more mouths the better! She even managed to wean some of the children onto a bit of spicy West Indian fayre.

The Janitor, Tony Shields, was there purely for his wage packet, he thought all the children were delinquent, and that all the house-parents were mad and perverted. He was never at work a minute before his start time, and no matter what the job is was doing, he would never just finish it off before he went home.

Then there was Grace, the tiny baby found in the room were her parent's murdered bodies had laid for several days. She had been covered in scabies, she was red-raw in a sodden, faeces and urine soaked nappy. She went to live on the Rose Tree in Willow House. She grew, went to primary school and she was happy.

Then one day, it was a Saturday in July, the sun was shining. She went across the estate and over to the woods near the greenhouses. It was there that the terrible thing happened. The thing that was the real trauma of her life. Murdered parents is one thing, and really, now she was ten years old, if no one had told her, she would not have known of their deaths. What happened on this sunny Saturday never left her. In an instant, in July, her world collapsed, it caved in upon her, it shadowed the sun and turned a happy girl into someone who could barely make it through a day.

Kevin Bradley was fourteen years old, he had been removed from his parents by order of the court. His father had done all manner of *Hammer Horror* things to Kevin. Some of the sexual things were repeated by various friends of this, so called, father. Unsurprisingly, Kevin had a view of sex and sexual encounters which was way beyond what the majority would consider to be normal.

Kevin had seen Grace. She was carefree, skipping across the lawn, still striped by Mr. Solms's careful mowing. He followed her towards the greenhouses and into the wood. Grace did not realise she was being followed. She found the tree she liked the best and climbed into the low hanging branch, she made herself comfortable and started to read her book. *'The Secret Seven'* jumped from the pages and she was soon in the heart of an *Enid Blyton* adventure. She did not notice Kevin, as he crept up until he was standing up right beside her. In a moment he had pushed Grace from the bough and she fell, as did her book its cover ripped. In another moment Kevin was sitting on top of her and covering her mouth. He had un-zipped his trousers before he pushed her from the tree, it was now his intention to push in between her legs and push himself inside Grace. In the struggle, and how she struggled, he hit her, he told her to be quite and everything would be over quicker. Grace still struggled; she tried to push him off. She failed. She was not strong enough or big enough. She felt the leaves and the damp of the ground against her bottom as Kevin pulled her knickers aside. She felt his hands touching her. She could feel his panting breath and she smelt him. She knew that for the rest of her life she would smell his smell, and she did not want that, but she could not hold her breath. She felt him touch her between her legs, no one had done that to her before, he was rough. Then she felt a burning right up and inside her. She found Kevin was pumping in and out of her and then he shuddered. She felt something red-hot inside her. He pulled away. She felt sticky liquid between her legs and she saw Kevin disappearing away out of the woods. She felt sore, and she felt filthy.

The consequences for Kevin came very soon afterwards. He was arrested and custodial sentence he was long. Actually he spent the whole of a short life in and out of borstal and Prison.

For Grace the sentence was life-long. Her crime was simply to be her, on a nice summer day, having an adventure with *Peter, Janet, Pam, Barbara, Jack, Colin George, Susie and Binkie 'The Secret Seven'* who were actually nine.

In her bed-sit above the kebab shop, with the picture of Sheikh Zayed Bin Sultan Al Nahyan's palace tooth-pasted to the wall, the smell of Kevin was never blotted out by the smell of Kebab. Even when the smell was the uncooked lamb-y version, as the shop was made ready for the evening trade. Kevin was always with her, his odour had filled her whole life. She never read *Enid Blyton* books after that fearsome day. She never felt happy again after that day. Oh yes, they gave her time with the psychologist, and they cared for her as best they could. The doctor had to check her over at the time, she recalled. She had not started her periods she was not pregnant, she had caught no disease -- but the doctor had to touch where Kevin had been. Grace decided then that no one would ever touch her there again. For a time she drifted through a smog of communes, with drink and drugs, it was hell. Until one day she found this little ledge, this little bed sit, and social services helped get her into it, and the smell of the kebab almost covered the smell of Kevin, and she had not to share a toilet. She stayed, alone. She never thought of herself as the baby whose parents were murdered, she knew that she was the girl raped by Kevin. Somewhere, sometimes, there was a glimmer that one day, some day, she might get to see the palace of The Sheikh in the Arab Emirates, but she decided not to hold her breath.

Chapter 50
Session Fifteen: If You had Not Loved Me
Kristopher

"Rose wrote me a letter." I started. "Oh, is she well? What about her daughter?" Replied the doctor.

"Yes she is but her daughter is not, she has cancer. You know Rose has had a tough life. Dad killed during Second World War; all those siblings; prostitution; first marriage failed and her second marriage ended when her husband is killed in Vietnam. Now her daughter is dying of cancer." I responded.

"I suspect she is made of the strongest stuff Kristopher."

"There is no doubt about that doctor, no doubt at all. Anyway, she wrote to tell me that she sent a letter to the enquiry. She wanted to make sure that my dad and mum could fall under no suspicion with regard to any wrongdoing on The Rose Tree Estate back in nineteen fifty-eight. She repeats what she wrote in a Christmas card she sent some years ago…... 'If you had not loved me I would not be able to love my husband and my children now.' Wow! That is something. Interesting too for it is in no way related to physical contact, I never once saw my mum or dad even touch anyone, not even on the shoulder, but people could feel the love around them. It was displayed in their care and consideration, remembering who each person was and what they were at Nut Tree House. Treating all with respect and dignity, even in fraught moments when dad had to be cross in order to restore order. That is something that not everyone seems to understand these days, people need to know where they stand, and if nobody pulls them up for wrongdoing, it diminishes their value because it says to the person, 'it does not matter what you do, it has no value'. It is an interesting letter, and quite out of the blue. I will write to Rose and say thank you."

"You're not into email and text then Kristopher?" Asked the doctor.

"Not when it is important, and this is important, to let Rose know that I am grateful to her and that what she has done is important. I have told her about our sessions and I have a feeling she knows something about my story that she has not yet felt able to share with me."

"There was another very interesting witness at the enquiry. His name is Anthony Lockhart. He lived on The Rose Tree Estate. Since then he has built his own demolition business. He had a contract to clear some old government storage building. He had been told that the building had been emptied but when he got into the building he found piles and piles of files. Many relating to The Rose Tree Estate. He even found a file with his own name on it! He also found a list containing his name with the letters PVOT written by it. This translated to Possible Victim Of Thacker. Thacker was the local Minister of Parliament, in the late fifties and early sixties. It was revealed that Thacker was a serial abuser who had done unspeakable things to many residents of Rose Tree, and to people from other care homes. Anthony told the enquiry that he was not a 'Possible Victim' but he was a geuine 'Victim of Thacker'. Anthony said that he was still afraid of Thacker, even though he knew he had died. Anthony said that there are some people who are just able to use the right tone in their voices, the right inflection and cadence, which convinces others that should you ever report, or your life will be as good as over. Anthony said he would never forget that voice, or the warnings it spoke, as he watched that man tuck in his shirt and do up the buttons on the fly of his trousers. Anthony said that is the vision is what he sees every night that he climbs into bed and closes his eyes to sleep."

Chapter 51
New Home Secretary
Narrator

The new Home Secretary, Julia Woodford, said to her cabinet colleagues. "My conclusions are these: Many children, and many young people who lived on The Rose Tree Estate, and in other institutions, did so reasonably happily. Many had been removed from horrendous situations, and their lives had been greatly improved by the care, surroundings, stability provided. By no means were all children and young people abused. By no means were all children or young people aware that some other children were abused. By no means were all the staff aware that abuse took place. There were many fine people who worked as house-parents on The Rose Tree Estate; they dedicated their lives to the service of the children. However, during all the years that The Rose Tree Estate was open, there were a large number of adults whose abuse of the children, in their care was, in my opinion, nothing short of evil. Each generation bought with it another wave of vulnerable people, and another wave of predators. It has to be noted that there were some adults, in every generation, who knew of the predators, yet they did nothing to stop what was occurring. Some did nothing for fear of the predators themselves or for the fear of losing their employment. It seems that not one of the adults who stepped forward to expose the crimes of their colleagues, remained in post.

It has to be said that, although The Rose Tree Estate helped many, there were many others were seriously harmed and let down by the care system that should have protected them. It is a scandal of the most ruthless and callous nature. In my view, it is not possible to undo the harm that has been done to so many. Although it is a poor compensation to provide money by way of recompense, as the Government we must, at least, provide financial compensation to those who have suffered. Colleagues, this statement is based upon the conclusions of the Chair of the enquiry. Her full findings will be published shortly, until then, what I have said to you today is to remain in this room. I thank you for listening so intently."

Chapter 52
Session Sixteen: Spiders
Kristopher

"I felt stripped bare, naked, and shivering as I heard what the man said. For as his words filled that enquiry room, it all became clear to me. I could feel the wild beasts thumping at the doors to the cages deep in the heavily guarded dungeons of my mind. In the haze I could see you, Doctor Samuels, sitting in your chair through all these long weeks and all these long hours, teasing these thoughts out of me."

"It was a fine sunny day and the sports day was in full swing, the sack race, the egg and spoon race, the wheelbarrow race had all been done. I had watched so much of it but something told me I was getting a bit bored of it all, so off I went on my tricycle. I was wondering what The Rose Tree Estate looked like when all the people it housed were collected on the sports-field; I wondered how quiet it would be. Eventually I came to the vegetable garden and the greenhouses. There was nobody there. I parked my tricycle by the water butt, I dipped my hands in to the water, it felt different to the water from the tap in the house. The gardener had explained to me that the water in the butt did not contain chalk so it was softer. Then I went into the greenhouse, I wanted to smell the tomatoes, I loved that smell. It was hot and sweaty in the greenhouse; I closed the door behind me. It was a big place, full of many plants and each had it's own scent. I was happy exploring."

"On one side of the greenhouse was a potting bench, made from slats of wood, it ran from one end of the greenhouse to the other. I could easily get under this bench, and crouch on the earth beneath it. I could look up and see the light through the slats. All along the brick wall, which was beneath the potting shelf, were air bricks, bricks with holes in them, these let in both air and light, and I could peer out and see the grassed-over space between the greenhouse that I was in and the second greenhouse about ten yards away."

"As I looked out I heard the voices of two people, a woman and a man, he had a strange voice, a foreign accent which I did not recognise. She was the girl who worked in the laundry. I could see them through the holes in the bricks, but not so very well, so I crawled along until I could hide behind the leaves of the vines, and from there I could see out of the window. Then I saw Ted from Hazel House, that was the house next along from Nut Tree House, I knew Ted, he was much older than me, and he sometimes played together. The foreign man, and the laundry girl were threatening Ted. They told him if he did not do what they wanted him to do, they would be straight down to Hazel House and let George, the house-parent, know exactly what Ted had been up to. Ted protested that he had done nothing. The foreign man said that it would not be what anyone thought once they had heard the story that Pamela was going to tell them. Ted looked anxious, he must have felt trapped. Pamela started to remove her clothes until she was standing there naked, she laid on a blanket and pulled Ted down beside her. She would have been better off undressing Ted whilst he was standing, but after some fumbling he was naked too and, by now so was the foreign man. It was just at this moment that I must have succumbed to the heat in the greenhouse, I must have fainted. I must have fallen to the floor. The *ménage à trois* were to busy and noisy to notice me."

"My dad found me, it was dark so he had a torch, he carried me back to Nut Tree House. He put antiseptic and a plaster on a cut on my forehead. He said we would collect the tricycle in the morning. I asked him if he would get it. He said that he would. I never went to the greenhouses after that, I could bring myself to be there again. I remembered what had gone on, but it is only after all your work with me, and what has emerged at the enquiry that has given me some insight. I do not know what to make of it now, I think I am in shock Doctor Samuels; you have let the beasts free. I do know I feel wretched for Ted. He is in his mid-seventies. He told the hearing that he had never had a girlfriend, he had never had any form of sex other than with Pamela with the foreign man, her French sailor, looking on, I know now his name it was Marcel de Lyon. She said it to him over and over again. If he is still alive he must be nearly one hundred years old by now."

Doctor Samuels was silent for what seemed an eternity. Then he said: "I presume you have given this information to the enquiry?"

"Yes, but they questioned me about the story, I think some were sceptical. There was comment that at the time of all of this I was not much more than three years old."

The doctor asked: "How did your counter their reaction?"

I replied: "I said this

'Incy-Wincy Spider climbing up the spout' down came
the rain and washed the spider out, out came the sun
and dried up all the rain, and Incy-Wincy spider
climbed up the spout again.'"

Then I asked would they like me to do the actions too. I said I had learned that nursery rhyme when I was at that age, and that if I could remember that why should I not remember other things? I said that one of the problems with society is that they do not take children and their childhoods seriously enough. The newspaper has a story about a three year old dialling nine, nine, nine -- thus saving the life of the mother who had collapsed on the floor. In the next breath a child's opinion is swept aside as being valueless.

There is the whole of it; each of us is valuable, and unless we understand the value of each one of us, and act accordingly, elites will always take advantage, and take more than their share of the bounty, which the world can provide.

I said to them that there is an enormous burden upon every child, for as children we have it in our heads that whatever happens is our fault, this is because we are at the centre of our own 'solar systems'. Is it any wonder that so many adults carry such burdens with them as I have done all these years? Is it any wonder that so many damaged adults go on to damage the next generation therefore?"

Doctor Samuels gasped: "Wow what did they say to that?"

"The room was silent. Then I picked out that newspaper from my bag, remember that headline? 'The Witch of Rose Tree Estate?' Then something amazing happened."

"What?" Asked the doctor.

"Rose arrived in the enquiry room. All the way from America. You know I had not seen her face-to-face since nineteen fifty-nine, but there she was and I recognised her immediately. Yes she was not the young girl that she had been back then, I have never seen a photograph of her, as I told you, photographs were rare back then, I never saw her on one of dad's cine films. There she was, she called attention to herself and asked if she might be allowed to speak. She then confirmed my story. She said that my mum had wondered where I was on that sports day, and my mum had asked Rose to look around and see where I had got to. She came to the greenhouses and all but bumped into Ted who was running towards Hazel House with tears in his eyes. She could hear Pamela and Marcel, so Rose peaked around the side of the wall and saw them, she said it looked like they were getting dressed, then they turned and came towards her, she slipped into the bushes and hid. She was not one hundred percent sure of what had occurred but she had seen enough in her life to put two and two together, the expression on Ted's face had told her the full story. Rose said that she was in shock and that she felt she had to get away. She said she ran back to Nut Tree House and went to her bed. It was sometime later that my dad came to ask if she had found me, and only then that she realised she had seen my tricycle next to the water butt by the greenhouses. The Chair of the enquiry made it clear that, according to various sources, Pamela had been responsible for many inappropriate acts of molestation, perpetrated on a number of different children, on The Rose Tree Estate. It had clearly been going on for a long period over a long period of time. Pamela had apparently died. She had been born in nineteen-forty, The French Sailor, Marcel who had been her mentor, had been born in nineteen-twenty and no trace of him had been found, despite extensive enquiries."

Chapter 53
Reynash
Narrator

Reynash met with The Rose Tree Survivors Group. He was a successful lawyer. He was mature and so smartly dressed. At first, the assembled group of survivors did not feel at ease. He took off his tailored suit jacket and hung it on the back of his chair. He rolled up the sleeves of his shirt. The he said: "Welcome, please sit down, we have not got all night. I am Reynash, I am a lawyer and I spend most of my time these days working on cases concerning human rights. I am here to help any, or all, of the members of your group."

Julian interrupted: "I am Julian, I work for the firm that works for the council empting the rubbish bins. I am a 'Waste Disposal Operative', a 'Dust Man', my ole man was one too!" Everyone laughed, he continued: "Judging by the cut of your suit I ain't got the kind of money that will be enough to pay your rates. Besides what would a lardi da, poshed up solicitor know about The Rose Tree Estate, let alone any of us?"

Reynash paused and looked around the room at the survivors, and then he addressed Julian.

"It is very nice to meet you Julian, and all of you. My first name is Reynash, my surname is Smith. I adopted my mother's family name so I am Mr. Reynash Smith. Of course I am not here to talk about me and my success or failure. However, I do see the need to provide some context." Reynash held up his right arm. It was dark brown and had some black hair upon it.

"I do have arms, which are hairy; I understand that the modern young people like to have it lasered away. Nonetheless, you can surely all see these round burn marks. The man who lived with my birth mother, when I was a baby, used my arm to stub out his cigarettes, when he ran out of room on my right arm he used my left." Reynash held up his other arm as well and he said, as a joke: "Please don't shoot!" The survivors laughed. "My other mother, who adopted me, worked on The Rose Tree Estate as a nursery nurse. She married an Indian man who became my father. She liberated me from The Rose Tree and I studied Law at Cambridge University, I have been in practice since nineteen ninety-nine. Now judging by all your youthful good looks, I think that many of you would have arrived on The Rose Tree after my departure from it. There is no concern about fees, believe me, they will take care of themselves. I will say this -- you that you will need representation if you are to stop the council, and the government, from wriggling out of their responsibilities. Of course it is up to you, you may not like my style and may wish to find someone else. You may still think you can represent yourselves. I would say that a united front would be the most persuasive way of going about what is likely to be quite a difficult task. Multiple complainants and endless numbers of people who have committed the most awful of crimes. There could well be criminal trails down the line, so if you would like my firm, and I, to be your representatives, please will you write your details down for me. Name, age, address, telephone and anything you might like to tell me about your own case. All will be confidential, the information will only be for me and the members of my team. Obviously it will take some time to visit with each of you to take statements and it will take a bit more time to plan exactly how to approach and deal with the matter. So let's get the ball rolling."

Julian walked over to Reynash and said: "I want to apologise, Mr. Smith. We have had so many people telling us this and that. Bedsides, the experiences many of us have had left us not wanting to trust anyone. I think you understand."

"Surely I do Julian, please call me Reynash."

Chapter 54
Mavis
Narrator

Mavis was born in the summer of nineteen fifteen. By the autumn of nineteen eighteen The First World War was passing it's dangerous way towards the history books; her father was one of the unusual men, one who escaped, with his life from the Somme, a fierce battle which saw most of his follows slaughtered. The love he had for his wife and daughter shone like the sun. Mavis soaked up that sun, and reflected every bit of it into her job of caring for the children on The Rose Tree Estate. Forty-four years she worked there. In all that time she moved between many of the houses and worked with boys and girls of all ages. From the babies to the stroppy teenagers. She was always professional, always kind, always gentle.

"Give kindness and you will get kindness back." She told the children. Then one day she heard a new house-parent shouting at one of the children, he threatened to hit the little boy with a cane. As he raised it in the air, Mavis lunged forward and knocked him off his balance. He fell, the little boy ran and Mavis picked up the cane and shouted at the man lying shocked on the floor.

"When the Board of Guardians founded this place in eighteen ninety-eight it was to be a place where children would receive kindly and homely parental care. House-parents were forbidden to use corporal punishment." Mavis glanced around the room, and when she was sure no one was watching, she bought the cane down hard on the man's leg. "If ever I hear that you have hit one of my little children, woe betide you. As it is, I will report this incident and I hope that you will be dismissed from your post."

Mavis worked on The Rose Tree Estate from the day she left school until she retired. Nineteen thirty to nineteen seventy-five. In nineteen ninety-five Mavis was living in a residential care home about three miles from The Rose Tree Estate. Each Monday her best friend, Yvonne, would visit. Today Mavis was distraught.

"Yvonne, I cannot believe what it says in the papers about The Rose Tree Estate. It is disgusting. Have you seen?"

"Yes and it has been on the television too." Yvonne replied.

"None of it is true Yvonne. No one would dare hurt my little children. How could they? It says some of these things happened whilst I was still working. I just do not understand. No one would dare hurt the children when I was there. There was that awful man; I hit him with the cane he was going to hit poor little Timmy with. He was dismissed. The report details all manner of evil sexual crimes. Yvonne, tell me they have it all wrong. Nothing, I tell you *nothing* happened to my little ones!" Cried Mavis.

"I am sure that nothing harmed the ones that were in your care whilst they were with you Mavis. The Rose Tree Estate was a big place there were hundreds of children, many houses, many places hidden from view. Some of the perforators threatened, some bribed and some just came and went. You remember there were so-called 'Aunties and Uncles', so-called 'friends' of Rose Tree. Apparently some of those do-gooders were involved. They included politicians, and tradesmen. Then there were workers on the estate, you must remember that woman who worked in the laundry." Said Yvonne.

"Pamela! Yvonne, you must not speak so. She was a very nice girl; she did get rather fat I remember. I often wondered what happened to that French boyfriend, Marcel." Said Mavis.

"He was an abuser too. Do you remember a boy called Ted?" Asked Yvonne.

"Well there were several Ted's over the years, Edward was a common name then. There was one sweet little boy called Ted in Hazel House, but I was never in a house together with him." Mavis replied.

Yvonne said. "Well apparently Ted was abused by Pamela and Marcel."

"I am sorry Yvonne, I cannot believe it all. How could I have been there and not known of these horrors?"

Yvonne Said. "It is really grim to read all that has been written Mavis. House-parents who beat the children with canes and slippers. One child reported that he was locked in a dark cupboard, and threatened so that he would not tell on that tall house-father, that one with the bald patch and glasses who was there just before you retired. He touched the boy's private parts and rubbed himself."

"Stop Yvonne, I cannot hear this. You never knew of these things when you were working at Rose Tree Yvonne?" Asked Mavis.

"I never saw any such behaviours, and no one ever told me of anything, not the children or the staff. It makes me ashamed that I did not know. Should I have watched more closely." Answered Yvonne

"I am in absolute shock Yvonne. I feel dirty, I feel as though I let the little ones down. How can anyone hurt a child? It was bad enough when the police arrived, in the middle of the night, with a little naked bundle wrapped in a blanket. Oh how many tears I shed seeing little bare arms where someone had snubbed out a cigarette, or where they had flea bites, or they were so malnourished they were just skin and bone." Mavis wiped a tear from her eye with a tissue. "I just cannot believe it. My life's work. Of course I do remember some of the horrid things that did happen when Joe killed Evelynn and put her in the dustbin and that boy Kevin who raped Grace. Then the awful day you found that boy Justin, fourteen years old, and he hanged himself. Yvonne, was he a victim of one of these paedophiles? There were a couple of teenage girls who took overdoses and had their stomachs pumped. How many of the children were not victims? Oh Yvonne, Yvonne." Mavis and Yvonne were in tears.

Chapter 55
The Hornbeam Boys
Narrator

Archibald Anderson bought discipline to Hornbeam House on The Rose Tree Estate. His method was to use fear to scare the living daylights out of his staff and the boys assigned to his care. Of all the boys to pass through Hornbeam, under Archibald's regime, five boys committed suicide and eight boys had served time in prison. Six others received community sentences. Four made a living by selling drugs. Three were alcoholic's and five were drug addicts who were homeless and lived on the streets. There were others who managed to find themselves jobs and successful careers. Some married. All of them bore the scars of the experience they had had under the 'Archibald regime' and some, who had suffered sexual abuse by him suffer from posttraumatic stress disorder to this day.

Chapter 56
Daphne's Interview
Narrator

Daphne had started life in desperate circumstances and was put into the care of The Rose Tree Estate before she had come to an age where she could remember anything. The whole of her first eighteen years of life were lived there. She did well at school, and she went on to study futher. Today she was having an interview for her first job as a professional social worker.

"So Miss. Lyons, I see that you had exceptional results from all of your studies. I wonder if you would mind telling us a bit about yourself. We have read your CV., of course, what I think we would like to know is, how you have hit upon the idea of looking for a career in this field." Said the women, who was leading the interview. She was so smartly dressed, with her blue-rinsed hair, smart light blue suit and was that a real sapphire and silver brooch? Yes it was. It had been a present from her husband for their twenty-fifth wedding anniversary.

Daphne was feeling a little nervous and she gripped the edge of the chair she was sitting on, hoping for moral support from the chair, which was already supporting all of weight. Oh my, she thought 'I am I dressed correctly?'

She paused and then began her story.

"Of my early childhood I have little memory. I never knew my father or mother. I know of no brothers or sisters. I know of no relatives at all. My first memories are of Willow House on The Rose Tree Estate. I grew up on the estate and lived there for the first eighteen years of my life. Then for two years I worked my passage around the world, doing temporary jobs, here, there and wherever I could. I travelled throughout Europe; I went to the Far East, Hong Kong, Singapore and then onto Australia. From there I crossed to America. I met many people, I did all sorts of work and I had a wonderful time. I found a place at university and I have my degree. Now I would like very much to get this job because I really think that it is something I can do. I have a unique perspective -- well maybe not unique -- I do not really know because there may be others who have already done what I now seek to do."

Another member of the interview team, a man in a slightly ill-fitting suit with glasses perched end of his nose and some straggles of hair trying to cover too much of his balding head, continued the interview.

"What an extraordinary catalogue of travel Miss Lyon's, few people have had such opportunity and you are still a young women. Did you complete this journey entirely alone?"

Daphne was a little bit taken aback for in the tone of the question was a suggestion that she might not have been truthful about her journey. Daphne said:

"Yes, I travelled alone, let me show you." She leaned over to her bag and pulled out a photograph album, she said: "Now where will I start? Look, this is a good one of course there are not so many pictures of me, I really wanted pictures of all the things I saw on my journey. This is me, in Egypt, I am on a camel by the pyramids, somebody took the photo for me. In this one I wanted to remember just how huge the train was that took me across America." The interview team thumbed the pages of the album and the other female member of the team asked:

"However did you get the money to fund the trip, and to be able to cross the Atlantic by ship on your return?"

Daphne smiled. "All my years on The Rose Tree Estate I saved my pocket money. I got Saturday jobs. I never spent money, money goes a long way when you know how to be frugal." So Daphne Lyons got her first job as a social worker.

There is a glory in that story that maybe does not balance out the horror of all we have discussed, but at least there is something A positive story amongst so many dark tales.

Chapter 57

Session Seventeen: Feelings

Kristopher

"So we come to the end of this Kristopher." Said Doctor Samuels. "What are your feelings now?"

"Well doctor, exhaustion or maybe it is relief that, with your help, I no longer have to keep all that you found locked up inside me anymore. Everything is out in the open; the secrets have been displayed to the world. I suppose my hope is that, in the future, no one will be held hostage by threats from those who seek sexual gratification by preying on people who are too young to absorb it's complexities. I fear though that society, as a whole, is still immature sexually, and I fear that that means that sex will still be something to be hidden, that is really what makes it dangerous."

Doctor Samuels guffawed. "Oh really Kristopher! It is more than half a year since we began this journey. You have shared with me many intimate items from your life. Slowly but surely we have unravelled the knots and uncovered the truth. That truth was not just confirmed by what is in your head, but by the society. Seldom, actually never, have I had a case where one of my client's issues has been confirmed in a public enquiry. When I ask what are your feelings now, what I really want to know is -- how do you feel to have understood the truth?"

I paused and thought through what he had said before speaking: "Well Doctor Samuels, overall I feel totally exhausted, I feel as if the tide has gone out. The adrenalin has poured away and I am left with that strange feeling as the endorphins subside. Yes we have discovered the mystery of the dreams I had, but, as I sit here, the absolute final part of the puzzle has just fallen into place. As a child, to dream of a fat, naked, women, even though I had never seen such a thing before -- but there was more. I now remember the touch of her skin, and I remember her holding me and making me touch her. She told me I was naughty, I looked up and saw the man and he was telling her to keep going. I was not just an observer Doctor Samuels I was abused! -- Then, I suspect, I fainted, and they laid me in the greenhouse. I also now think it was not just on one occasion when they did things to me. So you ask how I feel. I suppose I feel in a similar way to all the other poor children who were abused, and raped, by those who should have given them love and care. Actually Doctor Samuels, I really do understand now why these memories were buried so deep, and why I chained them in cages. Right now I am feeling sick, physically, and right now my head is spinning. I feel guilt. For if I had had the courage, I could have spoken out before now and maybe I could have saved other children from this monstrous, vile scourge. Maybe it explains why I never have had success in relationships. Then the question is; how much poorer has been my life experience because of what happened sixty years ago? I feel wretched, Doctor Samuels, I feel distorted."

Doctor Samuels said: "OK Kristopher, I think we need to see each other before our usual two weeks interval, I think the day after tomorrow would be ideal. I will call you on the telephone tonight and tomorrow.

Chapter 58
Survivors
Narrator

'The Rose Tree Estate Survivors Association' held numerous meetings. From the testimonies they collected, and from the documents they studied, they reached the conclusion that during from all the years the Estate was open from the nineteen fifties until the mid nineteen eighties there were probably more than sixty people who were responsible for what was termed as industrial scale abuse. The local authority, which was now responsible although it had not actually been in existence during much of that that time, agreed that it would be easier, and cheaper, (many saw that word cheaper as being yet another assault) to offer all who had been resident on The Rose Tree Estate during all those years, a sum of money to compensate them for being 'put in harms way'. With higher payments being made to individuals who were assessed to have suffered physical and/or psychological damage. Claims could be made over a two-year period, the council expected at least two thousand applications. The council paid out eighty of the higher-rated individual claims.

Members of The Rose Tree Estate Survivors Association held a meeting. The council leader attended. There were angry scenes and tempers were lost.

"I was a child in Ash House, I was there in nineteen seventy-six, I was abused. I have waited more than half a year, since the council announced the compensation deal. There have been forms to fill and questions to answer. I am telling you, ten grand, for what I and others in this room went through, is derisory!" Said one tall man with short, dark curly hair and dark brown skin."

A woman dressed in a sari continued the debate; "The council's lawyers are unwilling to pay out the ten thousand, they sent me two different offers. They are haggling, this is not street bazaar in Marrakech. When the council announced the scheme they said; 'no survivor will have to restate their experience of abuse in court to get compensation.' Well maybe not in the court. The council were expecting around two thousand claims for compensation, they have, so far received only half that number. Why would that be? Well, one look at the form would be enough to frighten many away. Rekindling old memories that they have locked down into the deep recesses of their minds. What I want to know is this: is there anyone on the council or has got one gram of empathy for these people?" Said a woman.

"Me, I can't understand how you, Mister Council Leader, can hang on to your job. You know what happened to us. Your predecessors in the various councils that came before yours let us all down, now you are doing the same. Ten grand is all you are willing to pay. Just ten grand! Then we have to wait and we get questioned." Said a white man in a south London accent. He waved a paper in the air. "Just look at question three – bear in mind that this paper was sent to me in the post with my name on the envelope. These forms are sent out to people who the council know lived on Rose Tree. Question three asks; 'Did you ever live on The Rose Tree Estate? Well is that a 'no brainer' or what?"

All the while that the rowdy meeting went on, there were heckles, cheers, boos and clapping. The air was hot and damp, condensation clung to the windows. The council leader tried hard to hide the fact that his head was thumping, he knew that he was heading for a migraine. He also knew that ten thousand pounds being paid to approximately two thousand people, together with administration cost, was going to make a big dent in the budget. He was also aware that if forms were not filled in properly and an adequate amount of, checkable, information were not verified, this scheme could be abused by people who were not entitled to benefit from it.

The woman in the sari spoke again: "What about other people who have sadly died before the public enquiry? What about those who will not get the compensation, however measly it may be, either because they have died, moved abroad, or just do not hear about it. You say that the applications will only be accepted for two years. This is the council trying to limit its responsibility and protect its budget. You know what? You're right! The council should not have to pay out, it should be the government of the country. The Rose Tree Estate is not the only estate, or children's home, where there has been abuse, it went on up and down the country. This is a national disgrace and the government should bare the responsibility."

A cheer filled the silence as the women sat down.

Then something happened which shocked every one of the people in the room. The council leader stood. He banged his hand on the table and shouted. "Order! Order! I have listened to you and I feel as if I am the accused in a murder trial. I understand your anger, I can understand your hurt."

The council leader was heckled: "Oh Yes!" "You don't feel nothin' mate! What would you know about living on the Estate? Go on tell me!" Agreement was shouted out from the mass of people in the packed church hall.

"Well actually quite a lot." Answered the council leader. "In ninety seventy-two I was taken, by a police woman, to Willow House. I was dressed in rubber pants and a small blanket. I, of course, remember nothing of this, but a Nursery Nurse called June took me in that night. It seems I was found on an underground railway station, my mum had thrown herself in front of a train. The police found a note she had written, she explained that she had failed to find help from the social services and she thought the best way to get me looked after was to turn me into an orphan. So it was, and here am. When you ask me what I know, believe me I know! I was there for eleven years. That is partly why everyone can claim some compensation. I am sorry for the distress that has been caused by the forms, but the council has to be accountable, not only to you, but to all who live within its boundaries. I am not against you, I am with you, and now I have to concern myself with this." He paused. "I have told no one that I am a former resident of The Rose Tree Estate. I have a feeling that there will be repercussions if or when I am found out. All I can say is that it was my intention to do something to help all of you; I hope that I have done so. I am sure that there is no way to keep this between us. However, I will not announce what I have just told you to anyone. The press are not at this meeting; it is just us. the 'powers that be' may never find out, that is basically up to you. All I can say to you is that the deal you have been offered is the best deal I could get I had never planned to take advantage of the scheme myself for fear that it may scuttle what I have tried to achieve for all of you."

Chapter 59
Monkey Puzzle
Kristopher

It may be that you, reading this book, have had no experience of a care system. For although many people do go into the system, relative to the size of the population few people encounter it. My perspective on all of this is, somewhat unique. Firstly I have a very good memory. Secondly at a very young age I was very free. Thirdly. I was not a person sent to The Rose Tree Estate to be looked after. My parents went there to care for those who were sent there. They obviously felt secure that I was in no great danger from some predator, either that or they were oblivious to the possility. (May be that is an aspect not explored thus far, I would guess that people, in general, did not expect to find such appalling things as described so many did not look for them). It was not that they did not care, I know that they cared for me. What is written in this story is for the main part, a factual account of experiences mixed with stories I have been told by others over the years.

Of course proper names and even the name of the Estate have been altered. If you were someone who lived on the Estate, you will know exactly the place I refer to, although I have blended other institutions into it.

There was deep wickedness; there was also love and kindness. It must be remembered that although bad things and harm happened to some, there were good people who helped and gave a start to the lives of many young people who may well have died otherwise. We may want all systems to be perfect, but sadly until society manages to produce perfect people to work in such institutions there will always be those who take advantage of the vulnerable. I would suggest that education, information, openness and helping people to have a good self-image is a way forward. Young people need to be informed and they need to have a system through which they can report wrongdoing. That will not be perfect either, some young people who would abuse that system for their own ends, just as much as some adults will try to abuse. What would be better is if we can build a society that is full of individuals who have enough respect for themselves that they do not wish to disrespect others. If you love yourself then you can love others. You cannot give what you do not possess. Remember that card which Rose sent to my parents? This phrase was also in the scrapbook presented to my dad at Rose's wedding: 'If you had not loved me I would not be able to love my husband and my children now.'

Rose often wrote to my parents from wherever she was in the world. After my mum had passed, she wrote to me. Of course, by this time, letters gave way to emails and text messages. Eventually they fizzled out. Before they did, Rose made a trip from her home across the sea to London, for the Enquiry. I met her, and some for her family, in a posh hotel lobby. We had a lovely dinner and spoke of the days past.

I am fully aware too that if you were a resident of The Rose Tree Estate your perspective is probably very different from mine. I had loving parents. However, I was at risk, just as you, may be even more so because of the freedoms I enjoyed back then. However, by standards in twenty first century Britain, my loving parents might well be considered to have been negligent. I would counter that by saying I have been a strong independent person all my days and I have never had to rely upon others to do what I have had to do. My life has been my life, yours has been yours.

I really was there, I hope that I may have bought you more comfort than distress in your reading of this account. You know too that Doctor Samuels managed to uncover the secret that I had hidden. That actually I had been abused. I do not think my parents had any idea that this happened, both of them passed away years ago, so they will never know.

There was a man, Henry, by name, who suffered greatly at the hands of a particularly callous abuser. The abuse began when is was about five years old and continued until he went to secondary school. He kept all the painful memories locked away in his head in the same way as I did. I asked him if he would be kind enough to read my manuscript. He did, then he went to the police and reported the suffering he had endured fifty years before. Never had he spoken of it to another living soul.

I liked it at Christmas time when the crib appeared near the gates of The Rose Tree Estate and lights were hung in the monkey puzzle trees. The snow came, the brass band played and carols were sung. I liked it in the spring when the blossom appeared on the trees. I liked it when it was the first day after the Easter holidays and the girls would wear their summer gingham dresses and their straw boater hats. I liked it in summer when it was bright sunshine and the girls danced rock and roll on the grass outside Nut Tree House. I liked the sports day and the races, and the feast afterwards. I liked the autumn and the preparations for the Halloween party. I liked the freedom that was mine in those times at the beginning of my life. All the things written in this paragraph were shared with many of you who were on the Estate at the same time.

There is good and bad all over, there will always be good and bad times for everyone, making the best of the good and minimising the bad is the trick if you can manage it.

Chapter 60
Outward Bound
Kristopher

In the summer of nineteen-sixty my dad and mum, my brother and I, and two girls from Nut Tree House went on a trip to Devon. We went in dad's car, we were quite crammed in. It had no seat belts. I have cine film but I remember the trip very well. We took the road through the New Forest. We stopped in a bed-and-breakfast overnight, and had a day on a beach by the sea where a swan swam in the low tide pools and the sun sparkled on the sea.

One of the girls smoked a cigarette and pushed the filter tip end out of the window from her seat in the back of the car. The boot of the car contained so much luggage dad had to tie boot with string leaving the boot lid slightly ajar. The 'dog end' of the cigarette must have still been alight and maybe the turbulence of air around the car had picked it up. Somehow the cigarette end entered the boot and before long some of the boots contents were on fire. My dad saw the smoke and flames, in is rear view mirror, and pulled the car into the side of the road. It was on and uphill slope and it was obviously and new stretch of road. We all got out of the car as quickly as was possible. My dad was first to the boot, he cut the string with his penknife and pulled out a bag of clothes which was on fire. He checked that this was the only part of the blaze. He stamped on the flaming bag, and when it was safe, we climbed back into the car and we continued our journey. There was no air-conditioning and no radio, and it was hot!

The point of the trip was to take the two girls to a summer holiday Outward Bound camp. Outward Bound was founded by Kurt Hahn and Lawrence Holt in nineteen forty-one. The Devon camp, Ashburton, was well established for boys by nineteen fifty-nine when it opened for girls. Hahn was an educator from Germany. In the nineteen-thirties he came under much criticism from the Nazi's and found himself in prison for some days. He was also Jewish, so in nineteen thirty-three he moved to Britain and started to work. He had founded two schools in Germany. and The United World Colleges. He also founded the famous school Gordonstoun. He took ideas from Plato and wished children to be surrounded by *'Fair works, sounds and beauty.'*

Earlier in this book, Dr. Samuels and I paid a visit to The Rose Tree Estate. I looked over the road from the sweetshop, to recap, this was the paragraph...

"Well I looked across the road just then, with all my memories, the facts, as I like to see them. I remember that as a happy place, but suppose another person came along with a different idea in their head, they might hear themselves saying. 'Abandon Hope All Ye Who Enter Here.' Or 'Arbeit Macht Frie', 'Work Makes Free'."

'Arbeit Macht Frie' was the sign above the concentration camp at Auschwitz during the Second World War.

My dad and mum taking two girls to an event which was made possible by a Jewish man who had escape the Nazis, and who could very easily have been sent to Auschwitz. I find is a powerful thought.

If you could have seen the grounds of The Rose Tree Estate you would surely have thought that you were surrounded by 'fair works, sounds and beauty'. I wonder if the people in social work in the nineteen-fifties had picked up on that idea. For surely life is easier when the surroundings are nice.

The surroundings in Devon were simply beautiful. I remember picking purple clover. We had not been there long before the girls were in canoes and paddling down the river in the beautiful sunshine.

I have film of this and the overriding impression is the smiles upon the faces of the girls.

Yes, bad things happen, they should not. Good things happen too and more and more good should be done.

Look up Kurt Hahn for yourself, and forget the media representation of Gordonstoun and its royal connection.

Hahn believed that adolescents possess an innate decency and moral sense but that these are corrupted by society, as they grow older. Hahn thought that education could prevent such corruption. Hahn had his faults too, we all do!

From my experience, helping young people to understand sex and improving the self-image of people are ways to help eradicate the evil that some awful people do. Education, and being able to stick up for yourself, or to know who can help if you are not powerful enough to stick up for yourself, are all useful. Although these are far from easy issues. If you respect yourself you are in a far better position to respect others.

If you love yourself you can give that love to others. That is the key, if we could raise a society where each individual was free of fear, where each individual loves and respects themselves, then all would surely love and respect everything and everyone around them. Abuse is not born within the vulnerable it is born in the self-loathing of individuals who have little or no self-respect. You cannot give that which you do not possess. You can only give what you are inside.

Those young women had the time of their lives at Devon Outward Bound in nineteen-sixty and of all the stories in this book, I will hold the image of them the most clearly.

Chapter 61
Session Eighteen: Black Eyed Susan
Kristopher

"Well yes,' I said to myself 'Get a Grip, you managed sixty years pretty well.'

I realise now I must take the bad things that have happened and turn them into good." I said, whilst the doctor wrote on the paper clipped onto his aluminium clipboard, he was using his gold pen, which caught the light, in spendour, every now and then.

"I met a man once, we were sitting on a park bench, a fine summer day. I started the conversation because I had noticed that the man was covered in tattoos. I have to say they were beautiful tattoos. He was much younger than I, and I remarked that all the artwork must have cost him a fortune. He told me that in ninety-eighty he had been removed from his family home and was placed under the protection of the social services and he went to live on The Rose Tree Estate. He said despite all the awful things he endured in his original home -- the wrench of being removed and separated from all that he knew -- was a pain equal to being stabbed by a knife. He said it was like falling into an abyss and I just kept falling. He stayed there until the estate was closed down. His right arm was not completely tattooed. I asked him what the motivation was for having all this artwork sunk into his skin. He raised his arm and he told me to look closely. He told me to look closely at the centre of a beautifully tattooed flower. He said that the flower was called Black-Eyed Susan. It had bright yellow-orange petals and a long stem with black in the centre. He told me that his mother's name was Susan and that all too often she did not even have one eye on him. He said whilst she looked away, his mother's alcoholic boyfriend stubbed out cigarettes on his arm. The centre point of the flower was one of the scars left by a cigarette. He said so the bad was turned to the good. He said the home he was removed from was hell, but to him The Rose Tree Estate was heaven.

"I remember a history lesson at school. The teacher went on about all the battles and how miserable everything was in the past. I found it difficult to understand, so I asked him 'if everything was all so terrible and bad why did humans keep making babies? Why did they not all commit suicide?' At first I thought he was going to bawl me out and tell me what a stupid little boy I was to ask such a foolish question wasting the time of my fellows. He just stood there, his bottom lip dropped a bit and not a sound came from him. Everyone in the class knew that he had no answer. Of course 'terrible' is a relative thing; if something today is better than it was yesterday, you may well see the world though a clearer lens than you did previously. One of the biggest mistakes of the current society is, and you hear it all the time on the television, everything is EASY. Nothing takes more than FIVE minutes to prepare. In my experience, life is not easy and things are seldom over in five minutes. Most things take a lot of hard work.

"This is just an observation; it seems to me that many of the generations younger than mine have realised it is very hard to change big things. If an earthquake occurs on the other side of the world, what can we do? If a government is elected and it is not to your taste, what can you do? There are so many big issues that the individual can do nothing about. So they look to see what they can do something about, for example, 'name calling', they get all hot under the collar on their social media and try to shift the dial that way. It becomes very difficult for an older person, like me, to open our mouths without saying something wrong or foe fear of offending somebody.

The issues we have discussed over these weeks though are things that need to be banished from every corner. I would say it should be a human right to enjoy a happy childhood in safety and love."

*

"Doctor Samuels. There is one last question I have for you."

What is it asked the doctor?

"I wanted to know, do you like the sound of a grandfather clock?"

ISBN 978-1-7396723-0-0

73747 Words

Lulach Publications

Lightning Source UK Ltd.
Milton Keynes UK
UKHW020647140722
405843UK00009BA/746